# PULP *Literature*

PULP LITERATURE PRESS

Issue No. 23, Summer 2019

Pulp Literature Press, Publisher; Jennifer Landels, Managing Editor; Melanie Anastasiou, Acquisitions Editor; Jessica Fabrizius, Story Editor; Daniel Cowper, Poetry Editor; Emily Osborne, Poetry Editor; Amanda Bidnall, Copy Editor and Graphic Designer; Mary Rykov, Proofreader; Kate Landels, Cover Design. For advertising rates, direct inquiries to info@pulpliterature.com.

Cover painting, *Greetings* by Akem. Illustrations for 'Wall Street at Night' by Chaille Stovall. All other illustrations by Mel Anastasiou.

Pulp Literature:  ISSN 2292-2164 (Print), ISSN 2292-2172 (Online), Issue No. 23, Summer 2019.



Pulp Literature Press gratefully acknowledges the support of the Canada Council for the Arts.

*Pulp Literature* is a proud member of the Magazine Association of BC and Magazines Canada.

# TABLE OF CONTENTS

# FROM THE PULP LIT PULPIT

## *First of the Summer Wine*

**The good old stories** are always imbued with a heady tincture of ancient elixirs. Sekhmet is pacified with a pomegranate-stained beer to quench her bloodthirst, Beowulf faces down Grendel in the mead hall, and you, dear reader, sink into our pages, pint in hand. Or are you elegantly poised, stem of a freshly poured piccolo of prosecco slipped between your fingers? Do you, like Odysseus, sail wine-dark seas of story?

Every season we step into our vineyard to cultivate the vines and select grapes ripe to bursting. We press them the old-fashioned way, massaging the raw pulp so the juices filter into barrels, where they compound and concentrate as we attend to small details — the label, the bottle, corks, and capsules. Each of the editors has their own favorite vintage, but all are structured with supreme care as we work to create a blend of tone and texture. Here we present Pulp Literature Press's Issue 23, vintage Summer 2019. Sit back, sip slow, and as always, enjoy responsibly. Turns out the Okanagan Valley is good for more than just grapes. ~ *Jessica Fabrizius*

$\mathscr{I}$N THIS ISSUE

Featured author **Kelly Robson** shows us that wine making is a labour of love, and sometimes hate, in 'Good for Grapes'.

**Matthew Hughes**'s magnum opus, *What the Wind Brings*, debuts aboard the Spanish galleon La Virgen, with an epic struggle brewing on the horizon.

Stella Ryman is ready for new adventures in *Stella Ryman and the Locked Room Mystery* by **Mel Anastasiou**, while Allaigna must make hasty goodbyes in the final chapter of *Allaigna's Song: Aria* by **JM Landels**.

It's a dog-eat-dog world — or wolf-eat-dog world — in **Christian Walter**'s 'Wolf, Dog, Sun', and **Zoë Johnson** reminds us to take stock of everyday miracles in 'Inherited Love of Unexplainable Things'.

Take a draught of heady poetry from **Casey Reiland**, **Raluca Balasa**, and **Alison Braid**.

**Lena Mahmoud** breathes new life into an old Palestinian folk tale with 'The Thieving Pot', and **Josephine Greenland** dissects a Thai myth in the Bumblebee Contest winner, 'Wife Giver'.

**Deborah L Davitt**'s protagonists hold out for as long as they can in 'On the Sixth Day'.

Come and get the good stuff in **Susan Pieters**'s 'Black Market', and see the dark(er) side of Wall Street in 'Wall Street at Night' by **Chaille Stovall**.

We have the two runners-up of the Surrey International Writers' Conference Story-teller Contest in this issue: 'Biophilia' shows us there's hope in **Margot Spronk**'s post-apocalyptic world, but not necessarily for humans; while **Deepthi Atukorala** takes us down an emotional rabbit hole with 'White Rabbit'.

Happy reading!
*Jen, Mel & Jess*

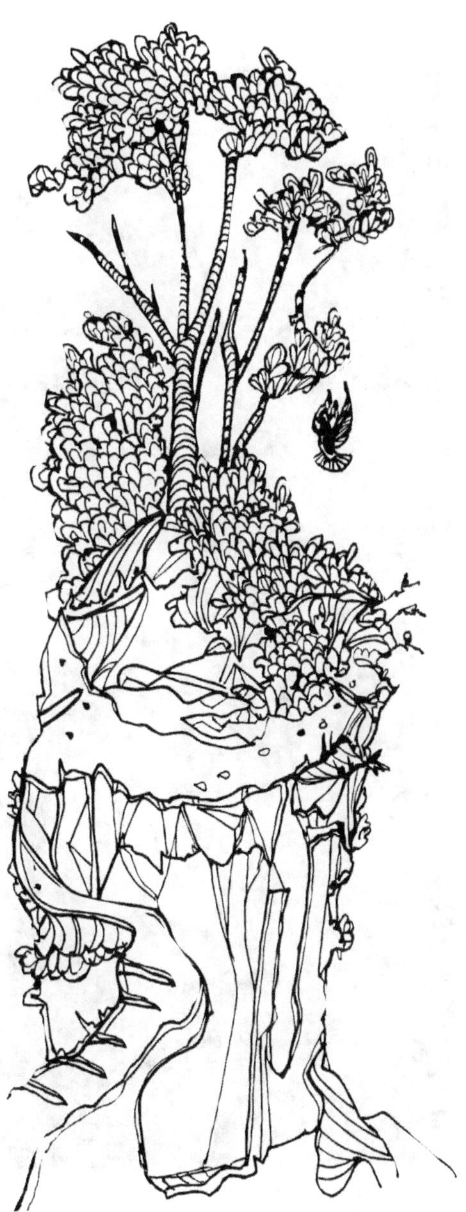

PULP
Literature
JJ Lee
'The Man in the
Long Black Coat'

PULP
Literature
Carol Berg
'Uncanonical Murder'

PULP
Literature
Matthew Hughes
'The Devil You Don't'
Mel Anastasiou
Carolyn Oliver
Eric Del Carlo
JJ Bergmann
Axel Robbins
Allaigna's Song: Aria

PULP
Literature
George McWhirter
'Stelk'



Allaigna's Song
Overture
J M Landels

PULP
Literature

FANTASTIC
FRESH
FICTION

www.pulpliterature.com

# GOOD FOR GRAPES

### Kelly Robson

*Kelly Robson* is an award-winning science fiction, fantasy, and horror writer. Many of her stories have been selected for year's-best anthologies and have been translated internationally. Kelly grew up in the foothills of the Rockies, competing in rodeos and gymkhanas. From 2008 to 2012, she wrote the wine and spirits column for Chatelaine. After twenty-two years in Vancouver, she and her wife, fellow writer AM Dellamonica, now make their home in downtown Toronto. You can find her on Twitter as @kellyoyo.

# Good for Grapes

**Simon wouldn't have set foot in Canada again** if the harvest hadn't been late. He'd badmouthed the Okanagan all over the world, from Coonawarra to the Cape, calling it a shithouse of overpriced land, badly managed vines, and wannabe winemakers who had no business being anywhere near a ferment. Threw it off, every time.

Nothing did more damage to wine than amateurs with money.

But California was early and BC was late, and when Simon got the email from High Bench Estates, he had just finished laying a Rockpile Cabernet into new French oak barrels, and he was planning to hit a Nicaraguan beach for a few months before Australia called him home to a hot February. But he had expenses, two of them, living with his ex in Melbourne. He'd emailed back with a jacked-up fee, and High Bench still wanted him.

So instead of surf and beer and stoned girls, he got a flight north and a long ride on a stinking Greyhound toward a valley full of no-hopers and vinifera trying like hell to ripen through frost.

Simon hunkered down in the back seat of the bus and tipped airplane bottles of rum into a travel mug. Just past Hope, the mountain pines turned from green to red. He probably wouldn't have noticed if the hippie kids in the next seat hadn't freaked out over all that dead forest. Pine beetles, apparently, killing trees by the millions. He listened to them whine about climate change for a minute or two, then plugged in his earbuds.

The French oak back in Rockpile cost over three grand a barrel. A few pennies too much to pay for wood, but Rockpile was a professional operation from rootstock to shoot. Simon had worked twenty-hour shifts coaxing the juice through a textbook ferment, and after a couple of years in those barrels, it'd bottle okay. The winery investors would be happy.

His ex had been happy, too, when he sent her the money he wouldn't be spending in Nicaragua. And High Bench — well, if the old man was going to put Simon through the wringer again, he'd just better hand over a fat cheque with a smile on his face.

**When the Greyhound turned off the highway,** Simon punched a text into the cheap burner he'd picked up at the Vancouver airport. The red truck was waiting for him. He remembered its antique fenders and peeling paint better than the two vineyard grunts lean-ing on the bumper. Huey and Dewey, he thought. Interchangeable. Both tanned deep brown but for the pale sunglass rings around their eyes and the white baseball cap stripes above their eyebrows.

Simon eyed the cuts and nicks knotting their forearms. "How they hanging?"

"Looking good," said Huey. "The Merlot was ready to come off three days back, but they said to wait."

Two minutes off the bus and it was already amateur hour. "Who made that call? Not the old man. His Honour would never wait to put it in steel."

Huey opened his mouth to answer but Dewey shoved an elbow in his ribs.

Simon tried again. "He didn't wait for winter last time. Nothing shy about him. Thought he could get a ferment from green grapes just by throwing in a pack of yeast."

Dewey grunted and tossed Simon's bag in the back of the truck.

Simon watched the rows climb past the truck window as they wound up the bench. The Cabernet Sauvignon on one side was throwing out suckers and cordons and big fat watery clusters, just like he expected. Bad farming, sloppy grapes.

The Cabernet Franc on the other side was only four or five years old. Nothing like the gnarled century-old Barossa vines he'd cut his teeth on, but they looked okay. Probably managed by a community college viticulture grad, doing it by the book. That would be fine until the owner decided he needed a higher yield. Then the kid would get canned and the vines would go to shit.

It was decent land, though. The slope coasted down to the lake, steep enough to create a nice breeze. Put it a thousand miles south and they might be able to make a bottle or two worth drinking.

"I bet the old man gets a gleam in his eye every time he drives down this road," said Simon.

Huey smirked. "The Franc belongs to a couple of Vancouver kids. They're going broke. And we're gonna get the lease on that rangy Cab Sauv. In a year or two High Bench will have all this land from mountain to lake."

"Be a shitload of work slapping those vines into shape," Dewey said, and spat out the window.

Simon felt a little sorry for the neighbours. Not for going broke—anyone stupid enough to put cash into Canadian wine deserved what they got. But nobody deserved the pain that came from tangling with the old man. He fought dirty.

Simon had worked a lot of crush pads. They blurred together into one cool expanse of concrete walled over with stainless-steel tanks and towering racks of oak. Three, sometimes even four harvests a year. California, New Zealand, South Africa, and Australia were in his usual rotation. Bordeaux and Tuscany now and then, just to pick up a few old tricks. Occasionally Washington or Oregon, twice Texas. British Columbia just the once. He'd sworn never again.

Most wineries left Simon alone to do his work. Only one owner had ever sat on top of him, poking him in the ribs and questioning his every move. At first Simon had ignored the old man and just tried to get on with the ferment. But it had escalated.

Dewey turned the truck onto a potholed lane. Simon got one glimpse of a new tasting room building before they turned onto a farm track dividing the blocks. He twisted in his seat and watched the estate spread out below as they climbed the mountain.

The Quonset hut was still there, set deep into the rock and shaded by a row of ponderosa pine. Even at this distance the fresh yellow paint couldn't disguise the rust around the joints. The landscaping around the new tasting room was still raw. Two cars and three motorhomes threw long shadows across the parking lot. The setting sun turned the valley rose and gold, the lake a long dark pool from bend to bend.

The vineyards stopped halfway up the mountain. A twenty-foot trailer was parked at the edge of the snake fence.

"You got the camper, that okay?" said Huey. "They said you'd want some privacy."

"It's a long climb from crush pad to bed," Simon said. Not that he hadn't slept on concrete once or twice.

"We'll leave you the truck."

Dewey dropped Simon's bag in the dust. The two of them waved and trudged down the track.

The trailer groaned under his weight, but it smelled fresh enough. The bed was made, the water tank was full, and some-one — bless them — had put six cans of Victoria Bitter in the fridge. There was a carton of eggs too, some milk, butter and cheese, and a loaf of bread beside the toaster. He flipped the safety catches on the cupboards. Coffee. More beer.

Simon added a dozen VB to the fridge and finished the cold stuff can by can, thinking how he should be on warm sand, watching tan lines wink at him from the brown backs of girls doing yoga in bikinis. He didn't look out the windows, not at the stars overhead, not at the lake below or the mountains between, and certainly not at the grapes that waited in ranks for the frost.

**The rising sun turned the camper** into an aluminum oven. Simon dragged a nylon lawn chair over to the snake fence and watched the light creep down the mountain. The first move-ment was in the campground off the highway — the harvest was worked by French-Canadian gypsies, if he remembered right. Just after dawn, they rolled out of their tents and headed down the road, six and eight to a car. An hour later the valley was busy as rush hour, harvesters and trucks working the wide flat blocks at the bottom of the valley, roped pickers stripping the vines on the steep slopes above.

But at High Bench, the only signs of life were the starlings squawking in the rows. Nobody working the harvest or even taking samples. The Quonset hut was deserted. No sign of Huey and Dewey. The whole estate spread out below him, so quiet it was almost spooky. He cracked a can and drained it, then got in the truck and drove downhill.

The tasting room door was locked. No surprise there — far too early to be waiting on tourists.

Footsteps sounded on the concrete behind him. A pair of big-eyed deer hopped over the fence. Simon waved them off. The deer trotted into the home block and began browsing on the vines.

"Pest management isn't my department," he said. But he ran the deer up the rows anyway, tossing pebbles at their flashing tails. He chased them over the drainage ditch and into someone else's vineyard — rows of Chardy that had been stripped weeks ago, the vines ravaged, leaves flyblown.

As he walked back down through the blocks, Simon had to admit the High Bench vines didn't look too bad. The fruit would never properly ripen, though. He plucked a few grapes, chewed them up, and spat the pips into his palm. The seeds were still green. No hint of telltale brown.

When he got back to the parking lot, the winery was still deserted. The Quonset hut was locked tight, its roll-down door secured with a padlocked chain. Simon ran his hand over the deep scars at the bottom of the metal door. The rust scraped over the pads of his fingers.

Seven years ago the door had been secured with two shot bolts threaded with heavy locks. Simon had hacked them off with an axe after the old man had locked him out of the crush pad.

Simon turned his back on the hut. He should just go back to the snake fence and drink beer until the old man came to find him. But there was no point in putting it off. And he wanted his cheque.

The track continued up a steep slope bordered by ponderosa pines, blocked by a metal gate marked *Private*. Simon dragged it open and left it swinging as he drove up the twisting switchbacks that climbed the ridge above the vineyards.

How many times had he stomped up this driveway on foot, angry as hell after a day of putting right what the old man had done wrong? The first time he had been sure of winning the argument, imagining he could beard the old man in his den. After a few more fights he began to learn that the old man never lost an argument. Nothing, not evidence, not education, not boots on the ground or a lifetime on the crush pad meant a thing to a man like that.

At the top of the drive crouched a house sharp and cold as a razor blade, a steel-and-glass box cantilevered over the cliff on a pair of iron beams.

Simon flubbed the clutch and the truck's engine coughed and died. He started it up again and pulled around back alongside the old man's hunter-green Jaguar.

This house was new. Seven years ago it had been a fake Tudor pile with flagstones and flower gardens, even a bloody grape arbour. Now no hint of the old house remained, its skeleton bulldozed into landfill and replaced by this thin slice of modernism.

One kind of rich man's dream exchanged for another. When this one got stale, the ponderosa pines would see a new dream form on the edge of the cliff, if the pine beetles didn't kill them off first.

The back wall was flat zinc siding, the door a slab of black marble. Simon knocked once, waited, then knocked again. He tried the door. It swung open.

Glass walls on three sides framed a panorama of valley and mountain and lake. An eagle's-nest perspective. No need for art on the walls when you're the lord of all you survey. The furniture was low, dark, modern, and uncomfortable.

The only thing out of place was the hospital bed.

The old man was on a respirator, his nose and mouth plugged into a plastic tube that snaked up from a metal bullet of oxygen on the floor. Swollen ankles puffed out above his too-tight socks, his paunch shrunken to a bib of flab under a sunken chest. The fingers of his right hand were stained yellow, but there were no cigarettes, no ashtrays, no hint of smoke in the air, just a faint antiseptic tang. The old man's fingers fiddled compulsively, grasping at air.

A plate of scrambled eggs and toast sat on a side table along with a photo of the old man in his younger days, stark as a raven in his judicial robes. A plastic water bottle was tucked into the blankets at his desiccated hip. Simon circled the bed. He picked up the bottle and held it out.

"Your Honour," Simon said. "It's been a while."

The old man fiddled the bottle with shaking fingers but couldn't seem to grip it.

"Not much there anymore." A woman's voice. Simon dropped the bottle and turned. She was sharp and sleek as the house.

"Nothing left of Dad but his habits," she said.

"I'm sorry——" Simon said.

"The fiddling." She twitched her long fingers, imitating the old man's gesture. "Watch."

The old man stared out the window. He lifted his fingers to his mouth, pursed his lips, sucked on air, and then lowered his hand.

"I always thought the cigarettes would get him in the end, but it was the drinking instead. Smoking's not going to hurt him now, but I'm afraid he'll burn the place down."

Simon looked around. "Not much here to burn."

"He could burn himself to death. But maybe that would be a better way to go. Liver failure isn't pretty."

"I can see that," said Simon.

"Dad went into diapers a year ago. He would rather have died right then."

The old man lifted his fingers to his mouth again. His eyes were glazed and unfocused, his jaw slack. A bubble of spittle hovered at the corner of his mouth. Simon walked to the window.

"You've got quite a view."

"You don't remember me, do you?"

He didn't, and that was surprising. She was pretty enough. But when he hadn't been fighting with her father, he'd been trying to save the ferment, even sleeping on the crush pad. And drinking, of course.

Simon shrugged. "It's been a while."

"Seven years. You fought Dad hard, and you taught him a few things even if he'd never admit it."

"Did I teach him to let his Merlot rot on the vine?"

"No." She smiled. Her teeth were very white. "That's my decision." She held out her hand. "I'm Marina, the judge's youngest. You don't remember me, but I remember you."

Simon shook her hand and turned back to the window. From this height he could see the big estate up the valley. Narrow orange trucks climbed the rows, tiny as ticks.

"Are you the High Bench winemaker now, Marina?"

"Not me. But I know what's good for grapes. Dad knew too, only he never applied the principle to the vines, just to his children."

"Your neighbours have the jump on you. Getting their harvest in as fast as they can."

"The weather will hold."

"The weather will hold?" Simon placed his fist against the window, clenched it hard. "You're playing chicken with winter. There's deer in your home block and starlings mowing through the rows. Get your harvest in so I can put the grapes in a fucking tank."

He said it too loud, but he didn't care. He was sick of amateurs and their magical thinking. The weather would hold, the ferment would take, and everything would work out. Well, she was paying for his advice, so he'd let her have it.

"Wine is farming. It takes hard work, not luck. You're battling the elements. And you know what? The elements always win. Making wine is chemistry. It's not art. It's not an opportunity for self-expression. It's science. Farming and science. You don't leave any of it up to chance or it's not a business, it's just a rich man's hobby and a fucking waste of time."

She blinked but didn't back away.

"I'll take care of the deer, but the birds are fine. They only nibble around the edges. The grapes want more sun, so I'm going to let them hang. And anyway, I was waiting for you."

"Waiting for me. Why? The old man would have hired a kid from the local college. Someone he could boss around."

"If you'll come downstairs, I'll show you. Bring that toast." She padded down the stairwell, bare feet on slate. Simon looked around, confused, and then his gaze fell on the old man's uneaten breakfast. As he plucked the toast off the plate, the room filled with the smell of shit.

Simon shook his head. "Your Honour," he said, "that's a hell of a sad way to go, even for an asshole like you."

The old man lifted his fingers to his lips.

Marina waited in the kitchen. A woman in scrubs was drinking coffee at the granite counter. At one look from Marina she put down her cup and trotted upstairs.

Marina unlocked a heavy oak door. "You're going to like this," she said.

"Is there a cellar down there?" Simon laughed. "Of course there is. Or do you call it the wine library?"

The stairwell spiralled down into a stone cavern lined with shining wood racks lit with pot lights recessed into rock. Racks of wine bottles were filed into alcoves with brass rack labels. Decanters and stemware gleamed above a marble counter with an array of corkscrews and decanting funnels and aerators. A digital humidity and temperature gauge blinked on the wall by the stairs, and the far end of the room was dominated by a towering, stainless-steel fridge vault. In the middle of the room, a pair of armchairs faced off across an oak table. The air was fragrant with yeast and leather.

"I call it the cave. I don't know what Dad called it. By the time it was finished, he couldn't really walk anymore."

"You've got a private cellar dug into the cliff, but you're still making your wine in a Quonset hut?"

Marina ran the rack ladder along its noiseless track and climbed up to fetch an unlabelled bottle. She looked at the slice of toast in Simon's hand and raised her eyebrows. Fair enough, he thought, as he bit into the cold toast. Let's do this right. Don't want to be tasting crap wine with a tongue fouled by beer.

Simon browsed the racks. One side was almost all Bordeaux, good labels and expensive vintages. Next to that was a rank of Barolo. Nothing wrong with the old man's taste. There were several dozen big spendy Napa Cabs further on, and then a rack of port followed by a dog's breakfast of local reds, vintages all jumbled together, some bottles past their time and most not worth drinking.

The other side of the room was devoted to High Bench wines, the bottles racked opposite the Bordeaux and just as carefully organized. The rest of the wall was filled out with vintage Champagne. Nothing wrong with the old man's ego, either.

Marina stripped the foil from the bottle she'd chosen and eased the cork. "We're not making wine in the hut anymore. There's a new crush pad built into the hill under the tasting room. Didn't you see it?"

Simon's mouth was full of dry toast. He shook his head.

"Well," Marina said, "it's nice. Everything you'd want."

He swallowed. "I can make wine in a garage if I have to."

"But don't you like it better when you have a proper set-up?" She turned her hand over and gestured at the room — a model's move, slow and elegant. "You can't tell me you don't like this. Be honest."

"Who wouldn't like it? It's a fucking wet dream. But it's in the wrong place. You can't make good wine here."

"Can't we?" Marina smiled. "Oh, I see. Tell me, what do you need to make good wine?"

All right, Simon thought. Kindergarten time. He resisted the urge to look at his watch.

"Good grapes," he said.

"Anything else?"

"If you've got a winemaker who knows what they're doing and a hardware store within a couple hundred miles, no. A few pieces of equipment would be nice, and an oak barrel if you're making red. But Sicilians make killer red in concrete troughs. It's not clean, but it's tasty."

Marina plucked a pair of stems from the cabinet and placed them on the table beside the unlabelled bottle.

"And how do you get good grapes?" She sat back in one of the leather chairs and crossed her legs.

"You farm the fuck out of them. And you don't grow them in Canada."

"Don't you? Well, you're the professional." She lifted the neck of the bottle to her nose and inhaled. Her eyes rolled back a bit, an involuntary gesture of pure sybaritic delight. If this was a High Bench wine, she was putting on a show. Either that or her palate was borked.

"Let me tell you how to get good grapes." She spread her fingers again in that model's gesture, inviting him to sit.

The scent of leather enveloped him as he sank into the big armchair. "What do you know about farming, Marina?"

She leaned back and crossed her slim legs. "I used to work in the vineyards."

"Sure. The vineyards at Tiffany's, maybe."

She smiled. "Since Dad got sick, I'm more in sales. But you remember me. Think about it."

Simon remembered a skinny teenager in coveralls and a baseball cap bringing in truckloads of grapes, working the sorting table, hauling loads of stems out to the compost. She had kept her distance at first, but as the fights with the old man got worse and worse, she started sticking close. He remembered her hovering at his elbow as the old man shoved his shotgun in Simon's face. He thought she was being protective of her dad, but maybe she had been learning something. Learning how to survive her father, maybe.

"Okay, farmer. Tell me what you think you know."

She leaned toward him. "Vines are generous. They want to produce. If you water them and baby them and let them get comfortable, they'll throw out canes galore and give you as much fruit as they can. But it's bad fruit. No flavour."

"Sure," he said. "That's Viticulture 101."

"So you torture them. Plant the vines close together so they have to compete for water and nutrients. Cut them back hard. Keep them thirsty and force them to drive their roots deep. Then you thin the buds until the vine is forced to put everything it's got into a few clusters just to please you. You don't get much quantity for your effort, but what you do get is the best quality. That's what Dad believed. Torture brings out the best. I know it better than anyone."

Simon sat back in his chair. "We still talking about grapes?"

Marina nodded. "What's good for grapes isn't so good for people. But I learned. I'm not sentimental. I don't baby the vines, I keep them stressed and make them work. And let me ask you, what's crueller than forcing vinifera to grow this far north? They beg for every ray of sun."

"If you're going to go crazy on me, better I get my cheque now."

She laughed and poured. A ruby stream tipped into the crystal, studding the lip of the glass like gemstones.

"Anyway," said Simon, "this isn't that far north. You're on the same latitude as Champagne."

"Now you're making my argument for me. No reason why we can't grow good grapes here."

"Go ahead. Grow Riesling and Gris. Cool climate varietals make nice little patio sippers. Bottle some fat Merlot and sell it at the grocery store. Make a sparkling if you want something to brag about. But you can't grow good Cab, and that's what you need to make real wine."

She pushed a glass toward him with the tip of her finger.

"Cabernet Sauvignon likes heat, and we have plenty. It's getting hotter every year."

Simon sighed. "You're the judge's youngest? I bet you never lost an argument, just like him."

"Dad lost plenty of arguments. Just never admitted defeat." She lifted her glass. "How about you? Ever admit defeat?"

Simon swirled the wine and plunged his nose in the bowl. The first whiff was pure black fruit, concentrated and treacly like a Napa Cab, but then all that fruit spread out over hot soil, sunk into good stony dirt. He swirled again and sipped. The fruit burst over his tongue and slid like velvet down his throat. The finish was plush with pepper.

Simon tasted wine all the time: tasted, measured, assessed, critiqued, and criticized. It had been years since he'd drunk wine for pleasure, but this glass practically begged to be drained.

He sipped again. "That's decent Bordeaux."

"It's not Bordeaux."

"Whose is it?"

"Yours."

Simon put the glass down. Crystal rang on oak.

"Ours," she continued. "High Bench, seven years ago."

"I never made wine here. Your dad did. I just kept his mistakes from turning into vinegar."

"Yes, you did. You gave Dad hell over it. Just one barrel of your own, the way it should be. The way you knew it could be. And this is it."

She sipped. Her eyelashes fluttered closed.

She could have been lying. Could have soaked the label off a thousand-dollar Grand Cru and poured him a big glass of bullshit. But no — she didn't just like the wine, she was proud of it. Proud like her father had been of his Jaguar and his big old house. Every sip seemed to puff her up just the way her father had puffed up every time someone down in the town called him *Your Honour* or gave him right of way at an intersection.

Ego, that's what he saw in her. Pure ego.

He tasted again. It was good. Very good, and after seven years starting to open up and even out. It would stand another ten years in the bottle, maybe even twenty.

He drained the glass and held it out. Marina refilled it, generously.

"Just one barrel, you said?"

"Yes, three hundred bottles. It's our Grand Reserve. We don't sell it, just give it away to wine critics and break it out for special guests. There are ten bottles left."

One barrel. Yes, there had been one barrel. Simon had slept on the concrete beside it, keeping the old man off it for weeks. In the end, he had stood over the barrel with an axe clenched in his fists as the old man shoved his shotgun's muzzle under Simon's chin. He'd panted with the urge to drive the axe blade through the old man's skull, his vision turning red at the edges. He had nearly done it, nearly scattered the old man's brains across the concrete, nearly painted the crush pad with his blood.

Instead, he'd shoved the shotgun aside and walked away. Went straight down to the highway, hitchhiked into the city, and got on a plane to Australia. Never thought about that barrel again.

But now here it was, good as anything, anywhere.

"One barrel," he said as she filled his glass again.

"You could make another this year, if you think you can do it again."

Simon swirled the wine. It clung to the crystal like blood and streamed into the bowl in thick rivulets.

Could he? He wasn't sure. Nothing in his experience could explain getting a wine this good from grapes like these. But he'd done it, somehow. Grand Cru quality. The kind of wine people search for, shed tears over, fight about. Legendary wine. His.

"All right," he said. "But I still want my cheque."

Marina stood and walked over to the fridge. "I haven't got it." Her voice echoed off the stainless steel. She opened the door. Cold air washed over Simon's skin.

"Fuck," he said.

"I haven't got the money," she repeated as she closed the door. "The new tasting room, new crush pad, this house. And the nurses, three shifts a day. Dying at home isn't cheap. But I'm talking to the bank again on Monday. "

She placed a can of VB on the table beside his wine glass. Condensation pearled the aluminum.

"The bank would be a lot nicer to me if I had a winemaker. A permanent one, not a hired gun. Someone to stay year-round, take the ferment from harvest to bottle. Especially if he was the one who made our Grand Reserve."

She was clearly crazy, Simon thought. He should grab the beer and run like hell. But there were only ten bottles left of his Grand Reserve. He could do it again, make more wine this good, or die trying.

Simon settled back in his chair and lifted the wine to his lips. "What the hell," he said. "It's only getting hotter."

# FEATURE INTERVIEW

## Kelly Robson

***Pulp Literature:*** You have some history with wine and spirits, so how long did this story ferment before you wrote it?

**Kelly Robson:** I wrote the wine and spirits column for *Chatelaine* for four years, which gave me a terrific opportunity to peer inside the wine industry. It's a very geeky world! Grape growing and winemaking are incredibly complex, and the people involved are hugely passionate. It's also a world of romance, land, and money, where you can lose a fortune very quickly. These are all great elements for drama.

'Good for Grapes' came together quickly. I loved being able to apply all the proprietary language I'd learned over the years, and to write about the heavenly landscape of the Okanagan.

***PL:*** Your writing leans towards horror and sci-fi; how great a role does realism play when you're imagining stories?

**KR:** I always strive for realism in characterization — especially in characters' emotional states, their prejudices, and their mistakes. I'll write in a consensus reality setting when the story requires it, but not all stories can be told, or should be told, that way.

For example, in my story 'A Study in Oils', the main character is fleeing his life on the moon. The lunar setting is a concrete metaphor for extreme toxic masculinity—what one reviewer termed "a Randian dream turned nightmare." Trying to write this story in a consensus reality setting would have been impossible. 'A Study in Oils' also suggests that in the future, indigenous people still have their traditional cultures and maintain a solid and meaningful connection to their traditional lands. I think that's a fantastic thing to suggest, and it wouldn't be possible in a consensus reality setting.

**PL**: What is it like being married to another writer? Do you keep your work lives separate, or is there a certain amount of collaboration?

**KR**: Alyx and I talk about story all the time. Things like: What is a great dramatic situation? How do we think about conflict? What is a story, anyway? And why do people always make such bad mistakes? These are the questions that fascinate us.

Having said that, though we're intrigued by the same things, every time we get deep into talking about plot, we end up going off in opposite directions. We're very different kinds of storytellers. But we are often each other's first readers. Alyx is an amazing story doctor, and I'm so lucky to have her on my side.

**PL**: Your novella *Gods, Monsters, and the Lucky Peach* has been nominated for several awards, including the Hugo and Nebula. What inspired that story and its wonderfully unusual protagonist?

**KR:** The story seed came from a Mesopotamia exhibition at the Royal Ontario Museum. One of the most intriguing items was a statue of a king carrying weapons which were specifically meant for killing monsters. Imagine this king. His whole job is to kill monsters to keep the kingdom safe, but he's never seen a monster. What would he think about that? How would that affect him? Did he know there were no monsters? Did he know the monster-killing stance was a sham at worst and a metaphor at best?

In the end, the story became more about the time-travelling humans whom the king sees as monsters rather than the king himself. Though Shulgi, who was an actual Akkadian king, is an important character in his own right and also as a story engine.

The main character Minh is an eighty-three-year-old ecological scientist. She is the epitome of the scientists I worked with in Vancouver for fifteen years—utterly dedicated to her work and convinced it's the most important thing in the world. Minh is not messing around. She's too old and tired for this shit. She just wants to get the job done. I find that a great dramatic situation, because a person like that is going to make a lot of mistakes.

*PL:* So many of your stories have been nominated for (and won) literary awards! Do you attend the ceremonies?

**KR:** I feel so lucky to have my work recognized in this way. When possible, I try to attend the ceremonies, first to show respect for the organizations that are supporting my work but also because it's exciting and fun. There are too few exciting, fun things in life to waste them. This year I'll be at the Nebula Awards in LA and the Hugo Awards in Dublin.

**PL:** We like it when authors give us stories outside their usual genres. If you were to change your genre, which one would you choose?

**KR:** Historical fiction, absolutely. I'm a huge history buff, and Canada has a lot of dramatic history that simply hasn't been done justice to. Could I write the Great Canadian Novel? I'd like to try, someday.

# WHAT THE WIND BRINGS

### *Matthew Hughes*

**Matthew Hughes** writes in many genres under many names, including Matt Hughes and Hugh Matthews. He has won the Arthur Ellis Award from the Crime Writers of Canada and has been short-listed for the Aurora, Nebula, Philip K Dick, Endeavour (twice), AE van Vogt, and Derringer Awards. Now he has pulled out all the stops for a foray into historical fiction, and we are thrilled to be his publisher for this endeavour. Here we present a brief excerpt of his magnum opus, What the Wind Brings, due out this August and available for pre-order now through our website: pulpliterature.com/product-category/novels/matthew-hughes/. You can follow Matt on his Patreon page for updates on this and other projects.

# WHAT THE WIND BRINGS

*Alonso Illescas*

**Today the sea is flat,** stretching away to the west like a dancing floor of green marble, veined and figured, until it meets a line that does not really exist yet is strong enough to demarcate world from sky. Yesterday, the wind blew fitfully from the south and made the ocean dance to its arrhythmic medley. The heavily laden galleon tacked continually, making scant progress as it alternately slanted toward the dense, forested shore with its strip of white beach then turned and beat its way out to sea again.

But today *La Virgen* has scarcely moved a furlong since the offshore wind died in the morning watch, like the last breath of a dying man, leaving … nothing. The sails hang inert, with not so much as a baby's fart to fill them. The expression is Mendoza's, speaking to Esquivel, the Basque mate, a moment ago. And now the stitched canvas actually billows a little backwards as the northbound current carries the galleon along against the resistance of the moist, dead air.

Alonso would like to know what is going on now as the captain confers with the Basque on the other side of the raised afterdeck, both of them staring fixedly at the south-western horizon. They must see something that eludes Alonso's unsailorly gaze, because some quality in the flat line has energized the two men. Mendoza is asking the mate a question, and Esquivel is tugging at the filthy ruff that rings his neck above the sweat-stained doublet. It is a habitual gesture; Alonso has seen him do it whenever the mate feels that responsibility is being thrust upon him. Esquivel will never be a captain, he thinks; he is a man always in need of someone to tell him what to do. He would make a good slave, Alonso is thinking, and then he turns the thought on its head and examines its other end. Does that mean that I am a bad slave, since I enjoy having a wider scope?

The captain has come to a decision, and now the mate is moving to carry out his superior's will. Esquivel is charged with energy now that the thinking has given way to doing. His shouts bring men running to the mid-deck, where *La Virgen*'s two boats are tied down. Hands untie and loosen the ropes on one of the boats, and in seconds it is turned right side up, revealing the oars stored beneath the thwarts. More shouts, all in Spanish but in half a dozen accents — Genoese, Venetian, Greek, even red-bearded Irish — more ropes, more coordinated bustle, and the boat is efficiently lowered over the rail to sit lightly upon the sea. In even less time, the second boat is in the water, and seamen are jumping down, seizing the oars. They row toward the bow, where their shipmates cast heavy lines down to them to tie to cleats on the boats' transoms.

Soon, Alonso sees the two boats pull out ahead of the galleon, the men at the oars bending and straightening in a slow rhythm, the wooden blades biting into the green-marble water, the thick, corded hemp tightening, spraying drops that sparkle in the sunlight as it lifts from the sea. Other seamen are brailing up the sails, and now *La Virgen* is turning, slowly, in a wide arc towards the open sea.

Alonso looks east to where a thin smear of green marks the unnamed land. Between the port city of Panama and the even newer port at Lima lies a realm of impenetrable jungle and muddy rivers that the Pizarro brothers have won from the barbarians for the glory of His Most Catholic Majesty, Philip of Spain. Alonso approaches Mendoza and says, "*Señor* Captain?"

Mendoza's back is to him. He looks south-west, squinting.

"*Señor* Captain?"

One of Mendoza's shoulders twitches beneath the heavy cloth of his doublet, but he does not answer.

Alonso speaks softly. "Why are we turning north-west? My *patrón* was very clear. The cargo is needed urgently in Lima."

Mendoza says something Alonso cannot hear then half-turns his head and says, "A storm is coming. There is no shelter on this shore. We must have sea room."

Alonso looks at the horizon then up to the sky, which is blue and innocent of clouds except for some high wisps far out to sea. He is not sure what to say, and so he says nothing. Things were clearer before they left Panama. *La Virgen* had been built for the Illescas in Nicaragua in the shipyards of the Gutierrez Brothers, a trio of shipwrights from Seville brought to the New World by the Illescas family. Don Alonso, Alonso's *patrón* and namesake far away in Seville, had seen that whoever owned the ships would control trade to the new and growing southern markets.

The Gutierrezes established a shipyard on the western coast after hauling their tools and necessaries across the isthmus by mule and on the backs of *Indios* conscripted by a conquistador turned *encomendero*. Don Alvaro Illescas, eldest son of Don Alonso and manager of the family's trading establishment on the sugar island of Hispaniola, needed the galleon to take a mixed cargo south to the port of at Lima. There the goods would be unloaded and carried up into the highlands, where the newly arrived viceroy was consolidating the *Audiencia* of Quito amid the spoils of the victory over the still-restless savages.

But two days before their intended departure, Don Alvaro had been struck by one of the fevers bred by the foul, damp air that hung over the raw city. He had called Alonso to his bedside, where he lay pale and sweating, while a priest who had training as a physician prepared to open a vein in his arm.

"Alonso," he had said, "you are young, but you must see the cargo to Lima."

"I will do it, Don Alvaro."

"I will send a letter with you to Jorge Estebar, our factor. He will deal with the authorities. Besides, the cargo is all paid for."

"Very good, *patrón*."

"But you must see it safely through. Sailors are thieves. Do not let them pilfer from us."

"I will not let them."

"And keep them away from the black women. They are not for the pleasure of Mendoza's sailors."

"I will sleep in the hold."

"Good. If any give you trouble, tell Captain Mendoza. I have already spoken with him."

The priest had cut the vein then, bringing a grunt from Don Alvaro and a spurt of thick blood that dripped from the elbow and into a wooden bowl that an attendant held, its inner surface stained dark. The sick man's face grew even more pallid. He reached with his unencumbered hand to take Alonso's, and the contrast of their skins, white over black, was stark. "Until you reach Lima, *you* are the House of Illescas. Act accordingly."

"I will not fail you or your father."

Don Alvaro blinked, and it seemed to Alonso that he would say more. But then a kind of haze passed across the man's eyes. He sank more deeply into the soaked bedding, ripe and rank with the iron smell of his sweat. The priest-physician put the fingers of one hand to the patient's wrist, while the fingers of the other brusquely fluttered to shoo Alonso from the sickroom.

*La Virgen* **moves sluggishly behind** the straining boats. Mendoza still watches the western horizon, now dead ahead of the bow. Nicaragua's coastal galleons are made mostly of cedar, not like the hardwood ships built in Manila for the trans-Pacific trade. She rides lightly on the water even though she is heavily laden. When her sails are filled with wind, the ship progresses to the accompaniment of a concert of her own noises: creaks of stays, tympanies of snapping canvas, the rush and gurgle of bruised water along her sides. But in this calm, there is no sound save for the shouts of the coxswains in the towing boats, calling the rhythm of the stroke.

The heat is stifling, the air so thick with moisture that, with every indrawn breath, Alonso can feel its weight settle into his lungs. The six passengers — two merchants and their wives and a blacksmith and a cordwainer — have come up from their cabins where they spend most of their days so as to avoid contact with the crew. Sailors are the lowest of the lowly, ranked down there with foreigners, and foreign sailors are doubly unacceptable. Alonso sees the passengers pull their sweat-soaked clothing away from their torsos, their faces red and dripping. The wife of one of the merchants wears a green gown stained dark down the back. Her husband notices Alonso and says something to his colleague. A brief glance in Alonso's direction, then both turn their backs and usher their wives farther forward.

Below decks the stifling heat must be worse. Alonso crosses the aft deck and approaches the captain. "*Señor* Captain, we should bring the Africans up."

Alonso always refers to the twenty men and seven women as 'Africans'. Don Alvaro and the crew of *La Virgen* usually call them 'the blacks', or 'the slaves', or 'the Moors'. It is important to Alonso to make a distinction, to draw a line between him and the people below his feet: they are of Africa; he is of the House of Illescas. He does not know what the sailors call him. He does not mix with them, nor do they approach him.

The captain is watching the horizon again. "Not today." Without taking his eyes from the horizon, Mendoza gestures toward the boats, full of his men, and says, "Who will watch them?"

"*Señor* Captain," he says again, "it is very hot."

"Let the blacks sweat. The storm will break the heat."

Alonso looks west. He sees no sign of a change in the weather. The high wisps of clouds are as faint as forgotten scars against the bland blue. He wants to argue with the captain, feels sure that Don Alvaro would not accept such a rebuff. But Don Alvaro is a hundred leagues to the north, and Alonso has already seen Mendoza order a one-eyed Greek sailor branded on the cheek for stealing from the food stores, blue smoke wreathing the end of the iron as the man screamed and fought a useless fight to escape the hands that held his head hard against the mainmast. Besides, it is not just the Africans Alonso is concerned for.

The merchants and their wives move farther toward the bow as Alonso descends the short stairway to the mid-deck. The main hatch is open, at least, though no air will be circulating in the sweltering space below. He stands at the top of the ladder, looking down into the darkness. The hold is a square of almost liquid blackness against the glare of light that freezes the deck. The smell of pigs' droppings rises, sharp and almost sweet. Usually he cleans the animals' pen while the Africans are on deck. He does not mind the noisome chore; indeed, the pigs are Alonso's pride. But he does not like to do it under the eyes of the Africans.

The hold is deep, and Alonso must descend to the lowest of three decks. For all it rules the deck above, the sunlight does not seem able to penetrate far. Alonso reaches the bottom of the ladder and stands in a twilight. He looks up, and now the hatch is so charged with brightness, he finds it almost strange to think he has just come from there. The glare brings water to the corners of his eyes. He has to suppress a sneeze.

The pigs rustle in their soiled straw, one of the little flap-eared sows making throat sounds that combine a snuffle and a string of grunts. Their triangular pen, a little forward from the ladder, is made of rough boards nailed to the ship's ribs and to a post that supports the deck above. There is no gate because the animals will not leave their sanctuary until *La Virgen* reaches La Portete. He strips off his much-patched doublet, rolls up the sleeves of his well-worn cotton shirt, and climbs over the top board. He reaches for the three-tined wooden pitchfork, nudging the animals with the toe of one brass-buckled shoe.

Usually they react to his arrival, rubbing against his shins, snuffling at his scent, talking to him in their throaty pig voices;

but today the terrible heat that fills the hold as if it could burst the ship's sides has rendered them torpid. Still, as he always does before mucking out the piss-soaked straw and lumps of pale excrement, Alonso stoops to scratch the young boar behind his ears, the beast's bristles stiff under his fingers. The pig grumble-grunts in pleasure, and one of the sows lifts her nose and makes a sound that could almost be a word. From behind him, deeper in the aft part of the hold, he hears a man's angry voice, a woman's softer tones, the words indistinct. Alonso does not turn to look that way.

He has known the pigs since they were month-old shoats on Hispaniola. "These will be the first swine to reach the newly conquered territories," Don Alvaro told him, "where they will breed multitudes. You are old enough now to have some responsibility, so these will be yours to care for on the journey. Feed them and keep them clean."

"I will, *patrón*."

Don Alvaro quirked his mouth, as he did when he was about to say something that he didn't mean to be taken seriously. "Years from now, when the new lands are thick with swine, you can say that you were the father of their nation."

Alonso smiled. From another man, it would have been mockery. But Don Alvaro was always kind to him, almost like an older brother. "Yes, *patrón*."

Now he scrapes the soiled straw to the edge of the pen, nudging the somnolent animals to move them, until the floor is clear. Then, with the side of a foot shod in the red leather shoes that were Don Alvaro's until they grew too scuffed and faded, he pushes the bedding under the lowest slat of the pen. He climbs out, goes towards the forward end of the hold, and returns with an armload of fresh straw, its dust tickling his nose, its sharp ends prickling the skin under his jaw. He throws the straw over the pen's top board, then makes two more trips until he is satisfied the animals are well provided for.

And, through all of this, eyes watch him from the shadows.

# STELLA RYMAN AND THE LOCKED ROOM MYSTERY

### Mel Anastasiou

**Mel Anastasiou** writes the Fairmount Manor Mysteries, the Hertfordshire Pub Mysteries, and the Monument Studios Mysteries. Winner of a Literary Titan Gold award and long-listed for the Leacock Medal, Mel is also the author of two illustrated thirty-day workbooks on story structure: the steampunk-themed The Writer's Boon Companion and The Writer's Friend and Confidante. For news on published and upcoming new works, visit her website, melanastasiou.wordpress.com.

Octogenarian sleuth Stella Ryman returns for her eleventh adventure with The Locked Room Mystery, wherein Stella comes face to face with a dodgy new character in the corridors of Fairmount Manor and investigates a baffling care home mystery. You can find the first two full-length books, Stella Ryman and the Fairmount Manor Mysteries and The Labours of Mrs Stella Ryman, on Amazon and at Pulp Literature's online bookstore.

FAIRMOUNT MANOR

# Stella Ryman and the Locked Room Mystery

## Chapter One

**On this first mid-morning in May,** Mrs Stella Ryman could not deny that her amateur sleuthing had today been of a disappointingly mundane variety. At Fairmount Manor Care Home, every day was much like the last, but Stella had successfully deduced that today was a Wednesday. She reminded herself that this was not an entirely useless deduction, for if her friends Thelma Hu, Theo Longbourne, or indeed any member of the Greek Chorus here in Corridor Park wondered what day of the week it was, Stella could clear the matter up for them without betraying their confusion to care workers or to the Director herself. She knew from personal experience how it felt to be labelled gaga, and she had suffered in spades the restrictions in personal freedom and stigma that came with it. Stella had not been allowed outside unsupervised since her arrival at Fairmount four months earlier.

But she had *escaped* more than once. And gotten away with it, too. Stella smiled at the memory. But past triumphs were stale bread in the absence of anything new to sink her teeth into.

This morning she felt edgy and far too hot for comfort. Golden warmth descended through the skylight over her chair in Corridor Park. To Stella's right, Thelma Hu tapped her cane against the floor in rhythm with her huffing sighs, and to her left the Greek Chorus set down their pillowcase crewel work to fan themselves with their hands.

In long lost days, the elementary school where Stella used to teach would heat up almost unbearably in May, and her youthful library helpers would scoot about the bookshelves and media storage areas in search of the long poles with special metal tips that opened the clerestory windows. In the meantime, the sun entered Stella's library office the way a ticket inspector entered a train car.

Now she was eighty-two. Stella no longer had an office, just her little bedroom called Room 34. She wondered darkly who now owned all the lovely things she had given up in her pre-Fairmount fit of finality. She had thought she was dying, and so it had seemed right at the time to proceed to a care home with no more worldly goods than a single suitcase full of brand-new coordinating fleece suits and knit tops, a few pairs of socks and underwear, and one faux painting of a farmhouse with ducks and apple trees in bloom, which she had purchased shortly after her eleventh birthday against her mother's wishes.

But Stella had not died. And she had spent February to April envying Theo Longbourne his cashmere cardigans and wishing she had kept her wool, silk, and cashmere school clothing. Now that May was here, she longed for the linen cotton shells she'd purchased from Lady Chapman's on Granville Street in every neutral tone, and which wore like iron and never gaped at the armholes. Stella grimaced and tugged at the short sleeves of the floral-print polo shirt the catalogue phone-woman had talked her into only a few short months back. *Something bright near the face takes years off, doesn't it?* Stella gazed down at her floral-print polo and reflected that in her real life she would have donated it unworn to the poor or colour starved. Even if wearing colours did take off years, it hardly seemed worth the sartorial discomfort to appear perhaps eighty instead of eighty-two. She wiped her brow with one short sleeve.

"Stella Ryman, can't you *do* something?" Iolanthe demanded.

"Yes, you think you're smarter than God's old auntie," Lucille said. "So what about handling this situation?"

The Greek Chorus scowled at her over the tops of their improvised fans. Stella met their frowns with a raised eyebrow. Of course, it was true that she had recently tracked down stolen goods, a missing resident, and the author of a set of very disturbing poison pen letters, but were Iolanthe, Lucille, and Sally not presuming too much about her personal powers?

Stella said, "You can't possibly expect me to change the weather for you."

Lucille sniffed and elbowed Iolanthe. "One minute she's more clever than the idiots that run this place, and the next she's gaga again." Sally the Nodder nodded.

"Stella, dear, nobody is asking you to adjust the direction of the sun's rays," Iolanthe said. "We're talking about that *room*."

Stella asked, "What room do you mean?" All the bedrooms at Fairmount were much the same except for the sponge painting on the corridor walls they opened onto: yellow for Daffodil Corridor, pink for Rose, and so on.

Thelma lifted her cane and poked Stella in the knee. "Everybody knows about the locked bedroom in Fern Corridor."

"But none of the rooms are—"

Iolanthe interrupted. "Who knows what could be inside a locked room?"

"A dead body," Lucille said. "A lurking murderer."

"Please don't worry yourselves. None of our rooms lock." She knew this was true for every one of Fairmount's bedrooms, because she had visited them all at one time or another in the course of her amateur sleuthing.

Iolanthe took a testy stitch in red thread. "Well, if you're not going to listen to us, Stella Ryman, at least you could have the decency to be deaf."

Ollie entered Corridor Park, pushing his cleaning trolley. He tucked his dust cloth into his trousers, set his hands on his hips, and beamed. "Well, lovelies, I'm here to swab the decks. Lift your feet when I get to you, and I'll try not to tickle anybody's fancy with my mop."

They all stuck out their legs in front of them. Ollie mopped under the chairs and down the centre of Corridor Park, humming to himself as he went. Lucille pointed out spots he'd missed, some of which were glaringly fictitious. As always, Stella admired Ollie's patience and jovial aplomb. Ollie was a care worker, not a janitor, but he kept the place clean anyway. Stella knew that Fairmount's director, Mrs Perdita Warren, was lucky to have Ollie in Fairmount's employ, and that she paid him extra for this custodial work. But not enough, was Stella's opinion, as he swabbed off around the corner in the direction of the dining room. She had no idea how much Ollie earned, but it would never be enough.

As if summoned by Stella's thoughts, Mrs Perdita Warren —aka the Warden—swept into Corridor Park. Her arms were full of paper flowers, and a stapler hung from an outlying thumb. She announced in bracing tones, "Today is May Day, and that's the day boys used to bring girls flowers, when you ladies were young yourselves."

"May Day?" Iolanthe inclined her head and took a stitch in her pillowcase. "I suppose that, in my time, I remember feeling a certain glow of expectation on the first of May."

Lucille said, "You could be sure as taxes that somebody somewhere would get kissed."

The Warden held out her stapler. "I've brought you ladies paper flowers to staple on the wall. Won't that be nice?"

An ironic silence answered her.

"Well, who would like to staple the flowers?"

Thelma said, "I'd do it, but I'm blind."

Lucille said, "I'd do it, but I'm sitting down."

Iolanthe said, "I'd do it, but our pensions pay Fairmount good money for somebody to do it for us."

The Nodder nodded.

The Warden set her paper flowers down on the floor beneath the bulletin board that faced Stella and Thelma. She tested her stapler by letting a staple fall to the floor for Ollie to clean up next time round, and said, "Well, I'll staple them up for you myself."

The Warden set to stapling paper lilies up on an empty bulletin board, her rear end moving rhythmically with the thudding click the stapler made.

Stella reflected that decorating Corridor Park must be a bit of an uphill climb for the Warden. For one thing, the bulletin boards above the Greek Chorus's chairs had been mysteriously bare of motivational posters for some time now. It was no mystery to Stella, however, because she and Thelma were responsible. They had been driven from apathy to outrage by such printed sentiments as *Hang in there, baby*, and *Talk is cheap but kind acts are priceless*, which had the nerve to be both smug and true. So she and Thelma had spent several evenings after lights out, rattling covertly down to Corridor Park together on sorties to rip down the damned posters.

The Greek Chorus set their needles and pillowcases onto their laps and peered up at the growing paper flower garden.

Iolanthe said, "Aren't lilies funeral flowers?"

*Staple-staple.* The Warden returned firmly, "They are *spring* blossoms."

Iolanthe said, "No, I'm certain lilies are meant to be laid atop coffins."

Lucille added, "Quick, somebody kiss me on the cheek and tell me I look natural."

Stella covered her smile with her hand. She felt more than heard Thelma's chuckle.

The Warden sent Stella a fierce look. "Do you have a similar complaint about the display, Mrs Ryman?"

"It's a lovely display. I've always liked lilies."

The Warden stapled a leaf to the board as if it had committed a terrible crime. "Don't be sarcastic, please."

"It's hard to be sarcastic about flowers," Stella said. "And anyway, I don't like sarcasm one bit. I was a teacher in real life, you know, and sarcasm in teachers is a terrible——"

"Of course, I'm always open to suggestions," the Warden interrupted. "But please do consider whether my university degree and experience in the field might not make me a little more qualified than you are to run Fairmount Manor Care Home."

Stella sat back in her chair.

Thelma leaned forward and poked the Warden's knee with the end of her cane. "*What* degree?"

*Staple-staple.* "Bachelor of Commerce."

"Oh, how lovely for you," Iolanthe said. "I myself have a master's degree in Art History. And Sally here is a bachelor of Home Economics, aren't you, dear?"

The Nodder nodded.

"*I* have a degree in refusing to tolerate fools." Lucille named a large bank. "I was a loans officer at the downtown branch for forty years. Turned down borrowers' applications for a golden thirty-three years."

Stella laughed. She couldn't help it.

The Warden slammed up an orange poppy so that its petals hung down on either side of the staple like a pinup centrefold. She sent Stella another freezing look. "I suppose you have a PhD in international law?"

Stella had earned her bachelor's in Education and a master's in teacher-librarianship, which information she decided it would be unkind to reveal just then.

Thelma said, "*I* have something."

Stella half-expected Thelma to disclose that she was a consultant to NASA.

But Thelma said, "I have a question. I want to know what's inside the locked bedroom in Fern Corridor."

The Warden replied, "Residents may not lock their rooms. There is no locked bedroom in Fern Corridor."

Stella might have forgiven the patronizing look the Warden sent Thelma's way if Thelma hadn't been blind.

The Warden said, "Now if you'll excuse me, we have a new

care worker on staff this morning, and I'm going to take him around Fairmount for orientation." She stapled up a final poppy and hurried away.

A new care worker? Stella couldn't see how Fairmount could afford more staff. Not without replacing present employees. Stella counted up the staff she and Thelma really couldn't do without: *Ollie, Cheryl, and Reliza.* Were they all present this morning? Had any of the Vital Three not shown up for work?

"I wish you were the director, Stella Ryman," Thelma said. "You'd do a better job."

"I'm sure I wouldn't," Stella said firmly, although it was just possible that she would. Certainly Ollie would do a much better job as director than the present Warden. Stella tried to imagine Ollie sitting in the Director's office, behind Mrs Warren's big desk, but she couldn't help picturing herself in that position of power instead, ordering better food for all the Fairmount residents, and telling off the Board of Directors for taking too much pay when care workers such as Ollie, Cheryl, and Reliza worked so much harder than anybody else.

Well, she couldn't do much about the food situation nor the underpaid, overworked care workers at Fairmount, but there was one thing she could do.

She would do it now. She slapped her hands on her knit-trousered thighs and got to her feet. "I'm going to find that locked bedroom in Fern Corridor and investigate it. Who's coming?"

The Greek Chorus blew out breaths. Lucille said, "That's hot work on a day like this one, Stella. You come back and tell us what you find out." Iolanthe and Sally the Nodder nodded.

Stella turned to Thelma. "You'll come, won't you?"

"No."

"Why in the name of little green apples not?"

Thelma scowled up at her. "Because if I show the locked room to you, then exactly what are you investigating?"

Thelma was right. Like tasty food at Fairmount, mysteries were not an everyday event. They were to be savoured.

Stella nodded. "I will investigate the case of the locked room and report back, then."

Iolanthe picked up her needle and pillowcase. "Take your time, dear. And then tell us everything."

Lucille added, "Don't leave out a single door handle."

The Nodder snipped off Lucille's thread.

**Stella wandered with intent,** if not with direction, throughout Fairmount's untrackable corridors, past the front office, the back garden outside the dining room window, Rose Corridor, and along her own Daffodil Corridor. She turned a corner at last that placed her in Fern Corridor. The green-sponged walls were quite restful, especially on Wednesdays, for (as earlier that morning she had detected) most of Fern's residents were off on a mall walk or watching television in the activities hall. She walked slowly, studying the slots on the doors, looking for one without a resident's name. If a room were locked despite Fairmount rules, she theorized that it was most likely unoccupied.

Sure enough, halfway along the corridor she discovered a door with an empty name slot.

She looked to left and right and tried the door. It opened. She stepped inside.

The room was empty of everything but the basic Fairmount furnishings: a bed, a visitor's chair, and a bedside table. The bed had been pulled away from the wall but was unmade, with sheets and a pillow laid out across the centre of the mattress. Stella checked the cupboard and the washroom, but both were empty and ready for a new occupant.

She left the empty room and returned to the head of Fern Corridor. She tried each door lever in turn, only to have every one of them click open to her hand. She said, "Hmph," and returned circuitously to Corridor Park. There she halted in the middle of the corridor, where she could easily speak to the Greek Chorus on her left and Thelma on her right.

She said, "I have investigated thoroughly ..." and paused, knowing that her investigative report would likely be the highlight of everybody's day and feeling unsure how best to communicate a negative result.

Iolanthe spoke into the pause. "You can see we're all agog. Please do tell us what was inside the locked room, Stella Ryman."

"I'm sorry," Stella said, "but I must report that there was no locked room in Fern Corridor."

The Greek Chorus stared. "Are you sure?" Iolanthe asked. "You didn't lose count and miss one door and count another twice?"

"Sounds like our Stella on an off day," Lucille agreed.

"I was very careful. There was no locked bedroom door in Fern Corridor."

Thelma said, "Baloney."

"With mustard," Lucille added. "On a soft bun."

Stella was about to make a very courteous offer to lead them to Fern Corridor and show them how wrong they were, when Mrs Perdita Warren gusted back into Corridor Park.

This time the Director had no paper flowers but brought with her a rather decorative man in a navy-blue care worker coverall. Stella thought he looked familiar, but she was aware that some people, even good-looking ones, had familiar sorts of faces.

Mrs Warren led the new care worker along Corridor Park. The Director named each resident for the new care worker, who greeted each of them politely.

Finally the Director said, "And this is Mrs Thelma Hu. She is blind and needs extra care, naturally."

Thelma said, "I'm not blind. I have macular degeneration."

"Of course, dear." The director of Fairmount Manor, aka the Warden, led the handsome new care worker away towards the dining room.

Stella turned to the Greek Chorus. "Did that new care worker look familiar to any of you?"

"Yes," Iolanthe said. "I thought he looked a lot like a young Clint Eastwood."

"No, I —"

Lucille interrupted. "Robert Redford, *Barefoot in the Park*, 1966. But with shoes on."

"I mean in real life."

The Greek Chorus shrugged.

Stella stood up and turned to Thelma. "Please show me the locked room."

Thelma got to her feet.

The tone for lunch sounded.

Iolanthe tucked her embroidery under her chair. "Did anybody catch that young man's name?"

"Mrs Warren didn't drop it," Lucille said.

"It seemed rather rude not to introduce us properly, I thought," Iolanthe said. The Nodder nodded.

"Now that you say it, I agree," Lucille said. "The Director named each of us, but she didn't introduce the new staff member to us in return. Strange."

"Not strange," Thelma said.

Stella nodded. She tried to put a finger on why the Warden's quick tour of Corridor Park had grated so.

Thelma did it for her. "When you take somebody through a museum, you identify the antiques by name, but you don't introduce the people to the antiques."

A silence followed, which Iolanthe broke with a sigh. "Yes, well … lunch, I think. It's a better use of time than murdering care home directors, isn't it, ladies?"

"Is it?" Lucille asked.

Stella said, "I could murder a sandwich, anyway." This was not quite true, because Stella would gladly have foregone the usual Fairmount luncheon to investigate more corridors with Thelma and see if they could find that locked room. But Thelma was as thin as a couple of sticks held together with string. She desperately needed every bite of food on offer, so when Theo Longbourne, with his blessedly excellent hair and gentleman's demeanour, came round the corner and offered the two of them his elbows for his regular Wednesday escorting to lunch, Stella accepted his left arm so that Thelma would take his right.

"How's your tinnitus? Any better?" Stella asked Theo. He had been a professor of music at the University, and she knew how he suffered with it.

Theo said, "Sorry, what was that?"

She nodded appreciatively at the joke. She explained to Theo the Warden's rudeness in treating them like museum pieces.

From Theo's far side Stella heard Thelma making small but piercing creaking noises. It was no use asking what the noises were about; Stella knew perfectly well that Thelma was pretending to be an un-oiled antique.

# CHAPTER TWO

**After lunch**—egg salad sandwiches with low-sodium potato chips, a favourite among the residents—Stella and Thelma set out along Fairmount Manor's twists and turns towards Fern Corridor. Their journey was a protracted affair, for Stella had no sense of direction and Thelma had only a thumbnail clipping of peripheral vision. They passed the activities hall twice, along with the stairway to Palliative Care, where she'd once discovered a friend in the middle of dying.* They skirted the front foyer three times. Once, Stella caught sight of a shadow in the doorway of one of Fairmount's many storage cupboards. The shadow looked very much like Mad Cassandra Browning, who was, for want of a better word, Stella's friend, even though Stella was fairly certain Cassie had died quite a few years before Stella had arrived at Fairmount. But when she dared to look deeply into the cupboard, she saw not Mad Cassandra but Dr Terry, in the storage closet he had commandeered for his work here. Dr Terry had parked his narrow behind on his swivel chair and laid his head upon a papering of files on his desk. He appeared to be deep in slumber. Stella knew that he was working through a time of heartbreak, for Stella herself had counselled the lovely

* 'The Fallen Crusader', *The Labours of Mrs Stella Ryman*

care worker Reliza to break up with him. It had seemed good advice at the time. Stella was not so sure anymore. But there was hope yet for Dr Terry and the lovely Reliza. Especially so, if Stella took a hand once more in bringing them back together.

So long as Reliza worked at Fairmount Manor, everything was possible. But what if the Warden, having overspent on staffing, must again cut personnel?

Stella dashed this worry from her mind. She would think instead about the mystery of the locked bedroom in Fern Corridor.

Stella and Thelma rounded another corner, and Stella braced herself for a third passage of the activities hall. Instead, to her delight, she saw that they had reached Fern Corridor, their destination. But they were not alone.

# Chapter Three

**Not ten feet away from Stella and Thelma,** two men faced one another. One was Ollie, Stella's care worker friend, and the other was the handsome new care worker. Both men wore their shoulders at a defensive angle, and each was talking over the other, so that it was all Stella could do to make out what they were saying.

Ollie: "Mrs Warren hasn't told me anything about giving you my keys, and I can't see why she would."

The new care worker: "Well, how should I know what Perdita told you, because I wasn't there when she talked to you, was I?"

Ollie, his hands deep inside his pockets: "If you've lost them, then get off your butt and look for your own" — Stella missed a word here — "keys."

Stella, a career educator, was well-equipped to sense impending escalation in corridor disputes. She and Thelma approached Ollie and the new man.

Stella said cheerfully, "Well, well, look at this traffic jam right here in Fern Corridor."

Stella could see Ollie was making an heroic effort to smile. "Stella *best sella*. And Thelma Hu! You're in Fern Corridor, ladies. Can I help you get home to your own rooms?"

The new care worker shifted his weight impatiently. Stella supposed that he was determined to take Ollie's keys from him. Well, Stella knew a little bit about determination as well.

She said, "I wonder if you two gentlemen would settle a bet."

Ollie said, "What's the bet?"

"Thelma says there's a locked room here in Fern Corridor. And I say there's never been a locked resident's room. Which is it?"

The new care worker shot his polyester cuffs. "What's at stake in this bet, lovely ladies? Then I'll know what side to take, because how else could I possibly choose between you?"

Thelma scowled in his direction. "You're *new*."

"I am."

"Already I don't like you."

Stella nudged Thelma. Thelma nudged back.

"Sorry," Stella said to the new care worker. "She hardly likes anybody."

"That's all right." The new care worker laughed. "I'll make you like me. I have my ways."

*I'll bet you do*, Stella thought. *You're the kind who has ways, all right.*

Again she thought she heard Mad Cassandra's ghostly cackle and the sound of her bare feet on Ollie's clean floor, just round the corner out of sight. But it was Reliza who appeared instead, moving in her youth and beauty towards Stella, Thelma, Ollie, and the handsome new employee.

Stella observed the new care worker's eyes warm with interest as Reliza approached them. She thought of Dr Terry collapsed in his nook of an office, wan with lack of sleep and love. And she remembered from her long-ago youth a fellow who looked very much like this one. He had appeared in the dance club Stella and her friends frequented, spiffy in a blue suit and shiny shoes. All the girls had turned bright eyes in his direction as he approached their table. He asked Stella to dance. She turned him down. When the others leaned across the white tablecloth and party-coloured drinks to ask her why, she had answered, "Trouble."

When she got to know him better, she discovered that her first impression had been correct.

She certainly wished she'd never married the fellow.

# Chapter Four

**Reliza clearly intended** to pass by Stella and the others gathered in Fern Corridor. The young care worker carried a tray laden with lunch dishes she must have collected from a bedridden resident. She nodded to the little group in a not-unfriendly manner and increased her speed. But the new fellow grinned and tapped her arm. "Don't walk too quickly. You'll make me look bad."

Reliza stopped. She adjusted the tray she held to prevent a melamine mug from toppling to the floor. "Do you need some help?"

"No, but you do," the new care worker answered. With gentle hands, he took the tray from her. "That's better. What's your name?"

"I'm Reliza." She reached out for the tray, but he pulled it away, and she put her hands in the pockets of her white smock. "Come with me, then," she told him. "I'll show you around the kitchen."

As the two moved away from them, the new care worker said his name to Reliza. *Riley.*

Stella had heard the name Riley somewhere, and fairly recently at that. The name resonated with the same sort of negative familiarity that his appearance did.

"Do I know that man?" she asked Ollie and Thelma. "Where have I seen him before?"

Thelma said, "You're wasting a perfectly good mystery. Why don't you investigate and find out?"

But Ollie scowled after the new care worker. "You don't know him. But you might have seen Riley when he dropped Cheryl off in his new car, before it was repossessed."

"So he's a friend of Cheryl's?" As soon as she'd spoken, Stella saw her error.

Ollie confirmed it. "Riley is Cheryl's husband."

Of course. Cheryl's husband. More precisely, the husband who had sold Cheryl's old beater and leased a luxury SUV for the family when Cheryl was wrestling with creditors, and who passed said lease off as a shrewd financial move. The husband whose SUV had then been taken back, and whose shrewdness meant Cheryl now had to take several buses to reach Fairmount.

*The husband Cheryl had left.* When Stella had heard that happy news, she had only just managed not to cheer out loud.

Now why would a wastrel such as Riley take employment at his ex's place of work for a care worker's small salary? What was more important to a spendthrift than money?

It was a disturbing question, for when money did not solve a problem, there were bound to be deeper, more dangerous issues in play.

# Chapter Five

**Reliza, and Cheryl** of the Giaconda smile and dodgy husband, excelled at settling residents in for supper in the dining room. Stella thought of them as the A Team. Of course, anybody could shoehorn an elderly woman into a chair, but these two talented care workers had the knack of making a person feel welcome and even valued. Almost as if this were a restaurant and they had actually chosen to eat here.

Stella said as much to the table. She asked Thelma, "If you could order anything, what would it be?"

"Moo shu pork," Thelma snapped back.

"Mushroom vol-au-vents," Iolanthe mused.

"Tomato aspic salad with pimento and black olives, created in a jelly mould shaped like a wreath, with mayonnaise filling the centre hollow," Lucille added.

Stella stared at Lucille. "That's one of my all-time favourites."

The Nodder nodded.

A companionable silent contemplation of dishes *d'antan* ensued, cut all too short by a fracas over at one of the Rose Corridor tables. A Nameless Dear care worker scolded two of the Rose ladies, who had apparently lost their medication. The former said, "This nonsense has happened too often. Where have you put your meds?" The latter protested that their meds were served to them with their meals.

The care worker huffed away from the Rose Corridor table, presumably to contact doctors for replacement prescriptions. Stella followed her progress out the door with an unfriendly eye.

Iolanthe waved her spoon at Stella. "Did you find the locked room after all?"

Stella shook her head.

"Have you given up?" Lucille demanded.

"Never." Stella picked up one of Thelma's thin hands and placed it upon her spoon, in case there was soup.

Thelma ran her fingers over the brightly coloured plastic tablecloth. She found her knife and fork and moved them closer to her plate. She said, "Well, maybe I was wrong about the locked door."

"You're never wrong."

Thelma cackled. "You're always telling me I'm wrong, Stella Ryman."

"Not *wrong*," Stella corrected her. "Just cranky."

"Then if being cranky is not wrong, I can be cranky all day long."

These were deep waters. Stella changed the subject. "Are these table covers new?"

Iolanthe said, "I asked a woman in Rose Corridor about these horrible plastic tablecloths. She said one of the care workers picked them up three for a dollar during the mall walk this morning."

Thelma tapped her cane against the aluminium table leg. "I still want to know what happened to our good mahogany tables. And chairs. *And* all the linens we used to have to go on them. Why are we eating bad food off plastic when we could be eating bad food off linen?"

Stella cheered up a little at the challenge of the problem. "Either the tablecloths were stolen, or they were put away. Were they worth stealing?"

"Only for ghost costumes," Thelma said. "Second-hand linens aren't worth anything."

"*I* know why used linens are so cheap," Lucille said. "They are too much work to clean and launder. No offence, Thelma."

Stella rolled her eyes. "Thelma was born in China, but that does not mean she ran a laundry, Lucille."

"I said *no offence*, didn't I?" Lucille shifted in her folding chair. "How am I supposed to keep up with race matters in a place like Fairmount?"

Privately Stella thought that Lucille might have kept up some-what better than this in her eight decades or so before coming to Fairmount.

The swinging door to the kitchen opened. Fairmount's cooks, Annie and Enid, placed bowls of steaming tomato-coloured soup on the steel serving shelves just inside the dining room, along with little bowls of soup crackers in cellophane wrapping.

Stella turned to Thelma. "I think you were quite right that there was a locked room. So what is the first question we must ask ourselves in the investigation?"

Thelma said, "The first question is, what's for lunch?"

"The cooks are giving us something red in a bowl," Stella answered patiently. "Now you answer my question. Why did you find a room locked one day and I found it unlocked the next?"

"Because I'm a crazy old lady," Thelma said promptly.

Stella frowned. "No, you're certainly not."

"I know, I just wanted to say it before *they* could." Thelma nodded at the Greek Chorus.

Iolanthe had the grace to appear embarrassed. "None of us think that, dear."

"What *do* you all think?" Thelma allowed Reliza to put a bowl of soup in front of her. "Why would the door be locked?"

"Well, what goes on behind locked doors?" The corner of Lucille's mouth crooked up. "Romance, that's what."

Stella regarded Lucille with new respect. She felt a little foolish not to have thought of romance. After all, the door led to an empty bedroom.

Reliza and Terry? But they weren't speaking to one another.

Cheryl and Riley, her estranged husband? This was more likely, unless you remembered that every second of a care worker's day was spent working very hard indeed under the gaze of a lot of bored elderly people. Stella said, "I think that if a couple of care workers were meeting up for hanky-panky, somebody would already be talking about it."

"I just did," Lucille said.

"But you made it up. That's not the same. That's like television: it's not a real mystery, it's just a story you invented."

"I want a real mystery," Thelma complained. "One where somebody commits a crime."

Stella nodded. "What crime?"

Care workers left bowls of soup and packets of crackers in front of each of them. Stella helped Thelma open the cracker package, feeling rather excited. She remembered earlier thefts from Mrs MacAndrew's treasure trove. But Alice MacAndrew was dead, and her granddaughter had her valuables now. And the bits and pieces that had gone missing in April[**] had not been taken for their resale value.

She came down to earth with a thump. *At Fairmount, what was worth stealing?*

Option one: nothing. Everything at Fairmount was pretty much tat, veneer, and pilled fleece.

Option two: something Stella couldn't see, like money in a bank account used to buy food like this red soup.

She wiped her mouth with a paper napkin.

A third option: something that seemed like nothing but actually was worth something to somebody. Her mind buzzing with assonances, Stella dipped her spoon quickly into her red-flavoured soup so as to finish up and get back to detecting the locked room as soon as she possibly could.

# CHAPTER SIX

**Stella ran her fingers along** the sponge-painted wall as she walked along one side of Chrysanthemum Corridor. Touching walls with fingertips was something she had done as a child, getting a feel for the properties of her world. The action served to keep track of the door levers she was trying, while her mind flitted restlessly around the question of extreme youth and age.

Her world was indeed small, like a child's world. And the perceived dangers, she saw, were much the same as they had been when she was little. Bathtubs, stairways, busy streets to cross … She had rebelled against them when she was little, and she

[**] 'The Ghost at the End of the Bed', *The Labours of Mrs Stella Ryman*

rebelled against them now. Coming full circle was meant to be satisfying, but actually it was no fun at all.

Full circle. She could see it all around her, a big grey circle, like a great tormenting wind, tugging at her. Pushing her down.

Stella put her hand on the wall to keep herself from falling. A fog of light filled the dizzying circle. It brightened the orange-sponged patterns on the walls to either side of her. She shut her eyes. She felt a knife-like jab of fear and self-doubt, like she had driven a car off the verge in a storm, and she wondered how such a thing could happen to a good driver like herself, and furthermore what was likely to come of it …

With the shiver that comes with a hard awakening, Stella decided that she couldn't stay one more minute in this place with so many doors and bedrooms. She must return to her own home and her own life. She wished to see her things around her, to cut May flowers in her own garden, and to walk to the corner store for milk, bread, and eggs. And why should she not? She knew her own address, of course, and even though she had come out today without her handbag, she kept a key under the terracotta moon face she had purchased in Mexico one spring break.

*Spring break.* School vacation must nearly be over. Time for her to get ready to go back to teach. It would soon be a new term, and she had her wardrobe to go through and organize for the next three months, when the weather turned so warm you almost had to go sleeveless. Thank goodness Jackie Kennedy had made shell tops respectable. Stella sometimes drew charts of her clothing so as not to wear her favourite ecru linen shell more than once a week.

She must get home at once.

Stella took a step into the bright swirls of orange and cream around her, but when she tried to take a second, the floor was not there. She reached for the wall, and couldn't find it. She toppled.

And somebody caught her. Long arms held her tightly. She found that she was leaning equally against the corridor wall and against the tall form of Theo Longbourne.

Theo looked down upon her, concern in his blue eyes.

Stella said, "Thank you."

"What happened? You look upset." He blinked, and she knew he was too kind to say, *Stella, you are crying.*

Stella wiped her face dry. As sternly as her mother Tanis Marie Seton would have said it, she reminded herself that she had sold everything she owned to come to Fairmount Manor. She had made her bed and must sleep in it.

"Stella, are you all right now? I was out for my walk …"

"Yes, perfectly." She made herself stand up straight. "Theo, what is there to steal at Fairmount?"

"In my experience …" He frowned. "Well, things do disappear out of my wash bag."

"Ah," Stella said. She closed her eyes, picturing the inside of a wash bag. "I didn't really mean toothbrushes …"

Theo didn't answer. She opened her eyes, and sure enough, he was gone, off on his walk around Fairmount's corridors again. She tried the bedroom door handle. It was locked.

It could mean nothing.

It could mean something.

*Nothings and somethings.*

Stella tried the last door in Chrysanthemum Corridor. She tried it again. A sense of excitement washed over her, and she pushed down once more upon the handle. It was locked.

She noted the door number: 42.

But how to remember it? At one time she would have pulled a pen out of her handbag and written the number on her wrist. But of course now that she was herself again, she knew only too well that she no longer carried a purse. No one did. There was nothing to buy, and just as the backside of one's fleece trousers stretched to contain as much rear end as the wearer might be equipped with, one's pockets held any amount of tissues and cough drops.

Stella took a tissue from her pocket and blew her nose. She tried the handle of Room 42 again and considered memory mnemonics. Six times seven was 42. *Room 42, at sixes and sevens.* Her mother Tanis Marie Seton now and then called out that phrase to Stella when she couldn't find her school books or she was late for the bus. *You're all at sixes and sevens today, Stella. Try a little harder.* Stella smiled.

*For once, you're wrong, Mother. Sixes and sevens are just what I need.*

# CHAPTER SEVEN

**When darkness began to look** less like a few sleepless hours before dawn and more like the far reaches of the eternal rest that must come to all, sleep-inducing games were ineffective. Stella had been through the alphabet twice (her favourite list featured TV series from the nineties: *Anything but Love, Blossom, Caroline in the City,* and so on) before she admitted that she needed to address what had happened to her in the corridor just before Theo had caught her and brought her back.

Had she had a stroke?

She pictured her mother as she remembered her in her eighties, tucked up in bed like Stella was now. Tanis Marie Seton's right eye and the right side of her mouth had pulled dramatically downwards. Stella touched both corners of her own mouth and articulated the small muscles there experimentally. She could feel no difference, but maybe a stroke was like insanity, and if you had it you couldn't tell.

If she *had* experienced a stroke, it must have been a small one. And a stroke meant permanent damage. Yet her lips and eyes felt the same to her touch as they ever did.

She turned over in bed and waited for sleep to come. When it did not, she listed TV series from the seventies (*All in the Family, The Brady Bunch, The Carol Burnett Show*) and then admitted that all those decades of entertainment and diversion had not lessened her worries one bit.

Because if she had indeed experienced a small stroke, she must face the fact that today was not the first time she had lost her place in the chronology of life. So several questions presented themselves.

First, how many strokes might she have had?

Second, how long would it be before a final great stroke carried her off?

And last, what if it carried her off before she solved the mystery of the locked room?

Stella sat up. Her duvet slipped off the bed. Her neck was sweating above the collar of her second-best nightgown. It was a warm night, and these were hot thoughts. She set her glasses on her nose, went into her little washroom, and with a washcloth wiped her neck, face, and the inside of her wrists. She gazed into her mirror and decided that her features were indeed no less symmetrical than usual. Feeling a little less shaky, she bundled her slippery duvet up off the floor and made her bed again. She looked from the bed, with its excellent mattress, to the door.

She pulled her door open and walked barefoot out into the corridor.

Despite the grit on the floors against the soles of her feet, and despite the nighttime smells of pine cleaner and (faintly) urine, Stella felt happy for the first time that night. The truth was that there was something magical about stepping noiselessly in grey half-light through places one was not allowed to be after bedtime. Again, like a child! In a tribute to extreme youth, she stuck out her tongue as she approached the open staff room door. Nobody saw her, for the room was empty but for several coats forgotten on their hooks, a testimony to the warm weather. Cheryl's threadbare jacket hung beside an expensive bit of rain gear that Stella thought must belong to the spendthrift Riley. Stella stuck out her tongue at Riley's coat as well.

So much for youth and silliness. There was grown-up work to be done. *Soldier on, Stella.* There were doors to be investigated.

She peered at room numbers and turned corners, right and left in turn, until she found herself before Room 42, which had been locked that afternoon. Would the door open? She held her breath. She pushed down on the lever. It opened, and leaving the lights unlit, she stepped inside.

She could just make out the bits of furnishings with which all Fairmount rooms were provided—visitor's chair and bedside table turned slightly out of place for cleaning. The clothes cupboard, faintly lit by the tree-shaded window nearby, showed vacant but for the shapes of empty hangers. The bed itself was like a black hole, with a slightly paler shape stretched down the middle. Stella stared hard, for her night vision was poorer than it had once been.

But she was almost certain that somebody was lying on the bed in this apparently unused bedroom.

# Chapter Eight

**The body on the bed** let out a wordless groan. The sound echoed in the barren Room 42. Silence followed, unbroken by any word or movement from the person lying in the darkness, or by Stella herself. Of course, groaning at night was not unknown at Fairmount, which was after all a building full of aged people who longed to go home; nevertheless, the sound was so chilling that Stella clutched the neck of her nightgown.

She wondered, *Man or woman?*

The person on the bed made the sound again.

*Woman.*

And not so much a wordless groan as a moan. The moaner's voice was rasping and oddly familiar. Particularly when the voice moaned out, *"Stella Ryman ..."*

Stella was certain of it now. The figure on the bed was Mad Cassandra Browning.

Stella switched on the overhead light. She blinked in the sudden brightness. "It's a bit much, *you* playing ghost, Cassie."

Cassandra Browning broke her corpse-like stillness. She cackled, wiggling her horny bare toes below the trousers of her purple velour tracksuit. Slowly she raised one hand aloft. Something hung from her fingers, twinkling and chiming in the light.

Stella strained to make out what the shiny thing might be.

*Keys.*

"Cassie, whose keys are those?"

"There is danger, Stella Ryman." Cassie jingled the keys again.

"Oh, Cassie, Fairmount Manor isn't dangerous," Stella said. "It's just bloody boring."

"Are you bored right now?"

Stella was not.

Cassie went on, "There is too danger. Wherever people are living, there is always a danger that they will die."

"Ha," Stella said. "Danger without adventure? I will grant you that."

"Adventure comes from inside you, Stella Ryman."

As if it were yesterday, Stella remembered comforting a third-grade child who was sobbing as if life were ending over the lost pencil her teacher had sent her to find. Whether your world was galaxy huge, elementary-school small, or the size of a minor care home, something immense was always at stake.

"Have you been locking Fairmount's bedroom doors, Cassie?"

Mad Cassandra Browning sat up. "Certainly not. I have better things to do with my time. Are you going to insult my intelligence, or are you going to solve a mystery?"

Stella asked again, "Then whose keys are those?"

Cassandra swung her legs over the side of the bed and dangled her feet above the floor. "The keys represent a clue, Stella. You like clues. I'll bet you have already figured out whose keys these are."

"I have not." But Stella realized that she had figured it out. She knew exactly who had recently lost a set of Fairmount keys. And if they were lost in this room, they certainly were an important clue — the first important clue, in fact, in the whole case. Room 42, first locked and then unlocked, was as important to the present mystery as she had hoped it would be. She must and would investigate.

Stella peered inside the empty wardrobe and washroom, but both spaces were empty. A few sad, empty prescription bottles lay in the bottom of the little garbage can by the toilet, but that was all to show that anybody had been here. Stella turned on the washroom light to take a closer look.

"Cassie, did you see who left those keys here?"

But the older woman didn't answer. Stella heard the slap of bare feet against the floor and then footsteps exiting the bedroom and hurrying along the corridor.

Stella left the washroom and followed Mad Cassandra Browning into the corridor. Cassie was spry for eighty-eight, indeed for most ages, but Stella herself moved more quickly than she would have believed possible. Her breath caught in her chest, and her left knee hurt like blazes, but damned if she'd let Cassie get away from her. She sped up again and rounded the corner to her own Daffodil Corridor by the staff room. There the door still stood open.

Stella stopped. She peered inside the staff room.

Mad Cassandra Browning was nowhere to be seen.

But one of the coats was swinging slightly, all by itself. She had previously determined that this was Riley's coat, the expensive bit of kit he'd left behind tonight because of the hot weather.

Stella glanced along the corridor, to one side and the other. She entered the staff room and moved quickly across it to the coat hooks. She fumbled inside Riley's coat pockets.

In one was a plastic prescription bottle. What drug was Riley taking, and for what ailment?

In the other were his keys. What if she somehow managed to make copies of them? What a talisman they would be to a sleuth.

Outside the staff room she heard footsteps, distant but approaching.

Stella replaced the keys and the bottle inside Riley's pockets. She was halfway out the staff room before she saw her error.

Detectives did not leave clues such as prescription bottles in the pockets of dodgy customers like Riley. And anybody trapped in a down-at-heel care home, hoping to solve mysteries and help fellow residents, ought to take gifts from the gods — or ghosts, such as Mad Cassandra — whenever they are offered.

Stella returned to the staff room and took back the prescription bottle and Riley's keys. She scooted back out into the corridor. In seconds flat, she reached her own Room 34.

# Chapter Nine

**Stella sat on the edge of her bed** in the dark, eyes closed, working to calm the frilly edges of panic that had accompanied her here. It occurred to her that she had two objects clutched in her hands that must not be discovered on her person. She turned on her bedside reading lamp and considered where to hide them.

How convenient, from a thieving point of view, that Riley's keys and empty prescription bottle were compact in size. Even in a room such as Stella's, where everything she owned in the world was either out on display for the casual viewer or inside her single chest of drawers, there must be places to conceal small objects. Unfortunately, she couldn't just bury them in clothing, for Reliza in her loveliness was apt to tidy residents' drawers for them, rolling socks and underwear into neat little ovoids that reminded Stella of owl pellets. Sometimes Stella felt mutinous regarding Reliza's obsessive rolling neatness, but just now she was glad of it.

She owned seven pairs of vari-coloured socks purchased at the same time as her knit tops. Two of her pairs of socks had gone to the laundry this evening, leaving five pairs inside her top bureau drawer. She tucked Riley's keys inside a floral pair. Of course the socks felt a bit on the hefty side, but there was no telltale jangling. Stella picked up a second pair of socks patterned with watermelons, inside which she would hide the prescription bottle, but first she decided to satisfy her curiosity. What was Riley on, anyway? It was sheer nosiness on her part, of course. And back in the real world, snoops were among the lowest of the low. But just as rock and roll musicians must bend now and then to accept the use of hard drugs among their colleagues, sleuths — even amateur ones — must remain open to investigating subjects that were arguably none of their business.

She peered through her glasses at the prescription bottle. The small print sent her over to her bedside lamp, where she squinted up closely to read the label. Nowhere did she see Riley's name. The prescription was for a well-known medication for anxiety. Of course, even a handsome man in his thirties might be anxious, especially one whose wife had recently kicked him to the curb, so to speak.

However, he was not likely to get such a prescription under the name *Joanne Gretcher*.

Stella read the name on the bottle again. Surely one of the women in Rose Corridor was named Joanne.

Stella was certain of it. And she was also certain that Rose Corridor had been mentioned at lunch. And hadn't she, the Greek Chorus, and Thelma Hu overheard a Nameless Dear care worker remonstrating with two of the women for losing their medication?

Slowly, thoughtfully, Stella hid the prescription bottle inside her pair of watermelon-patterned socks. She dusted off the bottoms of her feet as best she could, climbed back into bed, and lay awake in the darkness.

**Stella dressed,** washed her eyes, stashed the socks with Riley's keys in them into her pocket, and swung open the door. She was not at all pleased to find Riley himself at her door. He stood there smiling, one hand raised to knock. He held his other hand behind his back.

Had he missed his keys? Did he somehow suspect her?

Stella couldn't see how. "Good morning," she said coolly. "And how can I help you?"

"I'm here to help you," he replied. He had those raised wing-like eyebrows suggestive of depths of charm. Stella's husband had had those eyebrows, too. "Or rather to give you something."

From behind his back he produced a bouquet of flowers.

Stella eyed the flowers; there were roses in among the carnations, so they were not the cheapest a supermarket could offer. "Why are you bringing me flowers?"

"So that you will like me." The eyebrows rose to new heights.

Stella felt her heart melt slightly. *Damn it.* "Well, thank you."

He pulled back the flowers. "You're welcome. Do you have a vase? Shall I find one for you?"

She used to own at least a dozen vases of good quality, including a tall cut-glass one that would have been perfect for this particular bouquet. "Thank you. Very kind."

He winked and walked off with the flowers.

Stella spent breakfast wondering whether she oughtn't give Riley back his keys. After breakfast, she went back to her room to consider this question further. When she looked about her little bedroom and washroom, she didn't see a vase or flowers anywhere. She gave him the benefit of doubt and headed to her spot in Corridor Park. There she greeted the needleworking Greek Chorus trio and settled into her chair under the skylight.

At Stella's side, Thelma cleared her throat with a wet rattle. "What have you found out, Stella Ryman? Is there a locked room?"

The Greek Chorus set their sewing projects onto their laps and offered Stella their full attention.

Stella said, "There was a locked room. And then it was unlocked."

Thelma asked, "Did you go inside?"

"I did."

Lucille waggled her hands over her head. "Well, don't sit there like a chicken on her eggs, Stella Ryman. Tell us."

"There were three empty prescription bottles in the washroom garbage bin."

"Is that all?" Iolanthe asked. "I'll bet there are empty prescription bottles in everybody's room."

"That's all." Stella decided not to mention the ghost of Mad Cassandra Browning, since she was not completely certain Mad Cassandra Browning was a living woman after all. And she decided not to mention the keys she had stolen, either. She might tell Thelma, because Thelma could be discreet. But not the Greek Chorus, who might conceivably embroider the secret in red silk thread on pillowcases and wave them under the Warden's nose.

"Nothing else inside the locked room? Well, that's a disappointment," Iolanthe sighed. "No mystery at all."

"There may still be one," Stella said. "In the meantime, I want to ask all of you something. If a fellow gives you flowers, and offers to put them into water, and then does not put them into your room, does that mean that he couldn't find a vase?"

Iolanthe, Lucille, and Sally the Nodder exchanged knowing glances.

Before any of them could reply, Reliza rounded the corner into Corridor Park. She held in both hands a vase of flowers. Water sloshed around carnation and rose stems as she walked.

Stella said cautiously, "Those are pretty flowers, Reliza."

Reliza stopped. She looked down at the flowers with an unfriendly expression. "I don't think a man should give a woman flowers if he doesn't know her well."

Iolanthe said, "Oh dear *no.*"

"Riley should not have given these flowers to me. If he gave them to anybody, it should have been to his wife Cheryl." Reliza nodded. "I'm going to put them in the staff room so that all the care workers can enjoy them. It will send a message, I think?"

The young care worker moved away swiftly in the direction of the staff room.

*It will send a message.* What message had Riley sent Stella? Stella thought she knew.

She would bet her watermelon socks that Riley had learned from the Warden that Stella was the sort of Fairmount Manor resident that one could give flowers to with the knowledge that Stella would then forget about the flowers, and one could give the same flowers to somebody else, *viz.* Reliza. Thus killing two birds with one bouquet. Poor old brainless Stella, whose incautious heart might be won for a very satisfying moment with a phony bunch of supermarket flowers.

Stella heard herself growl aloud.

Thelma complained, "Was that a cat? I hate cats."

Stella raised herself up out of her chair. She made her way to Chrysanthemum Corridor, checked that she was alone at the door to Room 42, entered, and snatched the three prescription bottles out of the wastepaper basket. Out in the corridor again, she compared the prescription labels. Each of the three was written out to a different female resident of Fairmount Manor. And each was for a well-known medication for strong pain relief.

The discovery proved nothing.

But it sent Stella … *a message.*

These bottles meant that something was going on at Fairmount. Something to do with prescription drugs. She suspected Riley, but she disliked him, and that invalidated her suspicion.

She would have to investigate everybody.

Well, she had all the time in the world to bring to a new investigation. And she would begin today.

Two Nameless Dear care workers came around the corner, bearing between them bedding and rolls of toilet paper. One of them said, "Excuse us, dear, won't you?"

Stella stepped aside to let them into her room.

She looked down at her lightweight fleece suit and her lace-up shoes with their silent soles. Nobody could tell that she was hiding anything in the trousers' capacious pockets. She had to admit that, for investigative purposes, these unattractive clothes were actually better than silk and linens, stockings and heels.

She could never have hidden balled-up socks in a school skirt, nor moved in secret if she had to tap about the care home in three-inch heels.

She felt like Sherlock Holmes, disguised as a beggar in rags and tags. She felt like a human Purloined Letter, in full view but disregarded. She felt, in fact, ready.

She remembered Mad Cassandra Browning's words: "*There is danger, Stella Ryman.*"

Stella nodded thoughtfully. She shoved her hands deep into her pockets and touched on the keys to every door in Fairmount Manor Care Home. She walked towards the dining room for coffee and toast. She would need all her strength for the mystery ahead of her.

What had Thelma asked for?

*A real crime.* This morning, Stella could smell crime, as clearly as the aromas of breakfast that wafted along the twisting Fairmount Manor corridors.

§

*For more Stella, pick up the gold-medal winning* Stella Ryman and the Fairmount Manor Mysteries *and the recently released sequel* The Labours of Mrs Stella Ryman *from Pulp Literature Press or Amazon.com. pulp-literature.com/product-category/novels/stella/*

# AN EXAMINATION OF A FRECKLE

Casey Reiland

*Casey Reiland*'s work has previously appeared in the Headland Journal *and the* Puritan, *and she is the recipient of the Taube Award in Fiction from the University of Pittsburgh, where she received a BA in English Writing. Originally from a small town in central Pennsylvania, she now lives in the area of Washington, DC, and is on a mission to find the best pho restaurant in the city.*

# An Examination of a Freckle

The freckle on my neck,
      like a rough pebble soaked
            in muddy rainwater or
      a crumb of brown sugar
   found under the fridge,

clings to my cloud-soft skin
      the way my gray father
            grabbed my sister by her wrists
      as she slid down the steep
   bank to the cold river,

her lace-thin, boney arms stretched
      violin strings plucked and
            wobbling to the winter
      breeze, no cry escaping
   from her lips. I used

to scratch at the dark blotch
    hoping it would flick off
        like an eyelash or a pine
    needle fallen astray,
believing if I

shoved it under wet earth —
    the moist dirt crescent moons
        under my fingernails — a
    tree would sprout shiny leaves,
a green bruise healing.

My father dug up roots
    from weeds in our pond
        when the muck on the bottom
    dried and cracked open one
summer. My sister sobbed

as the fish wiggled their
    sleek, ribbon bodies, eyes
        smoke-covered windows. She
    begged for a flood to drown
our neighborhood,

a chance to kiss a sec-
    ond life. I am told that
        God molded me before I
    left the womb, but really
it was my mother's

hip bones that carved my chin,
       my cheeks, the knobby mole
              cradled near my collarbone,
         promising life stems from
   the weak legs of the

trembling fawn as my
       father picked him up round
              the belly, carried him like
          he was holding a glass
   doll or a vase of

seashells as I stood in
       the warm creek, the hairs
              on my pearl stomach suck-
          ing at the cool air, my
   hands open, waiting.

# WOLF, DOG, SUN

## Christian Walter

*Christian Walter is a German author, working across multiple genres. He lives in Switzerland but has also spent time in the United States and Mexico. He is a graduate of Viable Paradise and Taos Toolbox.*

# Wolf, Dog, Sun

> Wolf eats
> Wolf howls
> Wolf's insides eaten out

**Wolf drank.** That stupid playground chant. It wondered which demented kid had come up with it.

It ordered another. The bartender left the bottle on the counter next to Wolf's top hat. Wolf scratched the metal buckles on the hat band with its claw. The mirror behind the bar reflected the establishment's only other patron.

Dog leered. Its jowls dripped saliva across the table's scarred dark wood. Some got into the beer. It knew better manners. But who can help themselves?

Wolf took another sip. Heavy liquid burned its abused innards. It scratched its black coat, tried to ignore Dog in the mirror and behind. It rather liked the room's decor. Faded glory, not giving a shit. Not something it wanted to mess up. Besides, it didn't feel like dog meat today.

Wolf remembered eating the sun. It remembered the sound of horns, and how they made the earth shake right before everybody got down to the killing. Rivers of blood, mountains of severed limbs, blah, blah, blah.

Wolf was supposed to be down there. Amid the gods and monsters, deciding the fate of all worlds. It took a philosophical stance. They'd get it done by themselves. It was having a drink.

Another sip went down Wolf's throat. Smoke came out Wolf's nostrils. Dog was still leering. Wolf sighed. It got up to take a piss.

**Dog's head was jammed deep** in the toilet bowl. Well, what do you expect? Stupidity needs punishment. Call it Law of the Wolf.

Wolf leaned on Dog's neck a bit more, pushing him deeper into the bowl. Dog went in up to its chest. Its thrashing grew weaker.

Wolf took hold of one of Dog's hind legs, gave it a hesitant chew, sighed, spit it out.

Wolf pulled Dog from the toilet. Wolf threw Dog across the room. Dog bounced off the wall. Wolf walked across the room, stepped on Dog. Once, twice. Thrice for good measure. Wolf hunched down, muzzle close to Dog's wet ears.

"Why did you follow me?" Wolf asked.

Dog retched on the floor.

"Did you really think you could take me?" Wolf asked.

Dog retched some more.

Wolf sat down on the floor across from Dog. The walls were painted white up to the middle, red tiles to the top. Stalls to the left, urinals to the right, door in the middle of the wall opposite. Right where white turned to red, Dog had left a wet spot. Drops ran down the wall, like tears.

Dog said, "You ate the sun."

Wolf said, "That's right."

Dog said, "Now the world's ending."

Wolf said, "That's right."

Dog asked, "Why?"

Wolf scratched itself. "It's my job. Not the most pleasant one, mind you." Wolf said. It burped. Sparks struck the roof of its mouth. "But it's what I do." Wolf eyed its claws critically. Dog managed to sit up. Wolf kicked it over again.

"Will you kill me?" Dog asked.

"Yes," Wolf said.

Dog curled up and said, "Why? The world's ending."

"Because you are a domesticated motherfucker. Because you act as if you are not a killer. Because I find it insulting that you think you can come and get me in the goddamned toilet," Wolf said.

Dog raised its head. "I had to try. I'm a protector," it said.

Wolf roared. The walls shook. Dust trickled down from the ceiling. "Boy, you are stupid," Wolf said and dusted off its fur. "So tell me. What would you have done after?"

"After what?" Dog asked.

"Let's say you succeeded. I'm dead. What next?" Wolf asked.

Dog sat up again. "Release the sun, of course. End Armageddon," it said.

Wolf chuckled. "Like that is a good thing," Wolf said. It leaned in a bit. "You realize it has to happen. People took it as far as they could. Now it's a mess they can't fix. They long for this. Tabula rasa. Once everybody's dead, we start over. Like last time. You know that."

"No, I don't. And how would you know? You always end it in winter, when you're depressed. Everyone knows that. You don't give a shit about people," Dog said.

Wolf stared at Dog through slitted eyes. He hated the taste of dog meat. It made him want to vomit.

Dog jumped. Wolf slapped Dog down. Wolf stood on Dog's back. Wolf slammed Dog's snout into the ground. Teeth cracked and rolled across the floor. Dog stopped moving. Wolf got out a piece of rope. It thought of the taste of dog meat. The rest came easy.

**Wolf sat at the bar again.** A drink in front, a few more inside. It felt a lot better. Light filtered in through slanted blinds. Dust danced golden from ray to ray. The old wood creaked with pleasure where warmth touched it gently.

Outside, Dog ran yapping across the horizon. The sun trailed him on a bumpy ride across the horizon. Armageddon postponed. Wolf wondered how long it would take for the string to break, the string it had used to tie the burning sun to Dog's tail.

Wolf put on its top hat. Wolf grinned a fearsome grin. Wolf toasted itself in the mirror.

Happy birthday, fuckers.

# THE THIEVING POT

*Lena Mahmoud*

**Lena Mahmoud** is the author of Amreekiya, named one of Foreword's 'Four Phenomenal Debut Novels' of 2018 and described in Library Journal's starred review as "relevant for people worldwide." Lena was also a finalist for the Louise Meriwether First Book Prize and nominated for two Pushcart prizes. Her work has also appeared in Fifth Wednesday, Sukoon, and A Gathering Together, among others. For more information, please visit lenamahmoud.com or follow her on Twitter @lena_mabsutina.

# The Thieving Pot

**I was sure the only reason** Yama didn't want to take me to the suq was because she was ashamed of me. I had been in the family for generations as an inanimate, antique pot, but one day Yama held on to me tight and wished for a daughter. When my eyes formed, and I came to life, Yama was so stunned that she dropped me, and my newly animate body made a loud sound: *tunjur!* She decided that must be my name.

Still, people in our West Bank village couldn't decide if Yama, a single woman, was a sharmoota — a whore — or a majnoona, a lunatic. Most thought majnoona because I was a pot and had never been in her womb. She usually avoided people and their gossip, but today she needed to sell her embroidery at the suq and probably didn't want me there so she wouldn't look so strange.

"Ya binti, it's not that," she said as she folded her material on the floor, not even looking in my direction because she was so exasperated with my begging. "You're too young to know right from wrong, and I can't be watching you every minute with all the haraam things they have at the godforsaken suq." She went on with her lecture about how it was full of debauchery and thieving vendors, trying to squeeze every bit of money out of you. "I wouldn't think of going myself, but we need more than rice and lentils under your lid, ya Tunjur."

**Yama set me on top of the unlit stove** and made the journey to the suq, telling me not to leave the house. I sat there and stared at our crumbling walls, hoping that many would like the embroidery pieces she made; everyone in our village came to have her embroider their tablecloths, wall decorations, and dresses. Sometimes she also sewed; it seemed like Yama worked endlessly. I wondered why the other families around us were able to have meat at their dinner table and keep their houses warm so easily but those things were such a struggle for us to obtain. I suppose one needed a father to live such a life; having one must somehow guarantee that like magic, the way Yama's desire gave me thoughts, eyes, and a voice without her even being aware she could do such a thing. Yet somehow her desire couldn't give us a better home and food; she must have not wanted these things enough.

Hours later, Yama came back exhausted, her dark hair frizzed in a wiry crown around her head. She lay down on the floor and set the small cut of lamb beside me while she complained about the noise and the crowds she had witnessed only to sell half of her pieces. When she lifted her arm from her eyes, she noticed that I had not started cooking the meat. "Yalla, get on with it, Tunjur. My belly's as empty as a man's promise!"

I stared at Yama; I was disgusted by the sight and smell of the raw meat and tried to edge myself away slowly, sure that it would come to life and attack me. "Yama, I've never cooked meat. I don't know how." The last thing I wanted was that flabby red mess cooking inside me, contaminating every crevice with its stink and slime. I didn't understand why Yama had gone to such trouble to buy this.

Her pupils rolled so far back in her head that I thought they might disappear as she heaved her body from the floor. "I swear I must do everything. God won't give me an end to my work."

**After having the meat underneath my lid** for nearly an hour, I overcame my revulsion and decided I must have more, whether Yama would allow me the means or not. As soon as the first speck of sun shone, I was up and ready to sneak out of the house. I clanked along the rocky ground, trying to quiet the noise — *tunjur, tunjur* — I made, because if Yama heard, she'd be out in a minute to bang the lid against my body until I learned never to disobey her again.

After what seemed like more than an hour, I was sure that I'd missed the suq, but once I arrived, I realized there was no way I would have. Everyone was still setting up shop, displaying their wares and drinking coffee. I smelled spices, sweets, meats, and so many other things! I wondered what they tasted like. I saw a section with women selling embroidery and clothes, the older ones working on their designs at a frenetic pace while the younger women put the finished products out on display. I imagined these women were mothers and daughters, but after one long look, I walked away and went to the vendor selling dates, sweets, and honey. His face was brown and a little wrinkled, his black hair streaked heavily with grey. He told me his name was Abu Tareq, and he chuckled when I told him mine was Tunjur.

"What a fitting name for a pot," he said and then softly banged his fist against a coffee pot, sounding my name, *tunjur!* He picked me up and inspected me closely. He said his wife would love to have such an antique pot to cook the family's favourite dishes. I sampled all the food he had, and his son came out to admire my appearance. He thought I was just a myth, a figment of Yama's imagination a few old women and children were gullible enough to believe.

By the middle of the day, I was gorged with honey and dates, but I knew Yama would be running around looking for me, making more people gossip about how she was now more of a majnoona, yelling and screaming over her missing pot-daughter. I dreaded the walk back and the inevitable punishment; I knew I could soften her anger by carrying water from the well nearby and saving her a separate trip, or by bringing home a treat. Maybe some honey. That seemed easier, and more rewarding, than the water.

"What? You want more?" Abu Tareq asked, his eyes wide. "You took almost a quarter of my day's supply! Khalas. Enough for you. Maybe I'll give you some more in a few days."

I wandered around the suq and saw all the things I could never have or buy. The other vendors were not as generous as Abu Tareq. I hardly got a thing out of them, and I ended up having to hide when I heard Yama's panicked voice asking everyone if they had seen me. Most shook their heads while sucking their teeth to hold back laughter, though I knew they must have remembered me. I saw Abu Tareq tell Yama I had left over an hour ago, and I probably was at home by now. She narrowed her dark eyes suspiciously at him but walked back in the direction of our house.

The last thing I wanted to do was go back.

As the sun set, I walked back to Abu Tareq's booth and found him talking to a woman in the back while his son packed up their wares in the front. This woman was too young to be his wife but was probably too old to be his daughter; he leaned in close to her, and I saw longing in his eyes. I clanked over, placing myself in the middle of them, and looked up at Abu Tareq.

He looked down at me and sighed. "Ya Tunjur, why are you out still? Your mother has probably gone insane by now."

"Yama's already insane." I turned to the woman, who was smiling nervously at me. Abu Tareq explained who I was, but she only seemed interested in making a getaway as soon as possible.

Once she was gone, I asked, "Oh, who is she? She can't be your wife."

He clicked his tongue. "'Ayb! For shame, little girl. Don't say such things." His eyes were going a thousand different places at once; he was about to replace Yama as the majnoon of this village.

"I won't say anything if you give me a pot full of honey."

"No one will believe you," he said.

"Oh, the people of this village will believe anything, especially about haraam things going on between a man and a woman." I never got out much, but I heard Yama discussing those kinds of rumours on countless occasions. "Imagine if her father finds out." I paused. "Then your wife. I've never met Imm Tareq, but I bet she'll cut off your balls and feed them to you. I'll even boil them for her."

He glared at me and called out to his son to bring more honey. He grumbled as he poured it underneath my lid, calling me a shaytana, because what else could a pot brought to life be? And Yama was probably a witch, too, releasing such evil upon the village.

I clanked my way home with more vigour than I ever had before.

**Upon my return,** Yama yelled at me as she emptied the honey into the jars we had around the house. Her feet were sore from running around the village and the suq; I had disobeyed her; and, most of all, how the hell did I get this honey when she knew I had no money and the only person who saw me was Abu Tareq? He didn't mention anything about giving me any of his wares, not for free.

I took my place back on the stove to relax. "Ya Yama, you should have seen me! Everyone thought I was so beautiful and strange that they all gave me gifts and let me have some of their stuff. That's how I got all the honey."

She eyed me even more suspiciously than she had Abu Tareq and reminded me again that I had nearly killed her with worry. "So you're a novelty item at the suq now, not my daughter?" When I didn't answer, she said with a long, voice-cracking sigh, "At least you brought home a treat."

That night, after our rice and lentils, we feasted on the honey until I was glassy-eyed and Yama's teeth — the ones she had left, anyway — ached like a wound.

**After a week,** I decided I wanted more than sweets; I needed something that gave me long-lasting satisfaction. I realized that all the vendors had some secrets, and the ones with the most expensive wares had the most to hide. I only threatened to expose these secrets when they were truly humiliating and would bring me a good profit. I found out that Abu Dawood, one of the jewellers, gave out high-interest loans to people who had fallen on hard times; though many owed him money, no one found out that he did this so often, because they were too ashamed to admit their desperate situation. Besides that, he and his family occasionally ate pork. Who would want to buy their jewels from a pig-eating usurer? So every week, he gave me a pot full of jewels to stay quiet and keep his customers.

Abu Farid, the butcher with the most succulent cuts of lamb and beef, supplied Abu Dawood with the occasional cuts of pork he claimed he only sold to Christians, and sometimes he did not bother to drain the blood from his animals, the halal way. Thus, he made his customers sinners without their knowledge. So he gave me his best pound of beef and lamb every day.

Abu Farid gave me my cut reluctantly, but Abu Dawood did anything he could to avoid giving up his. He tried to get my sympathy, saying that he had a wife, four children, and a sick mother to provide for; he had little to give up. I always sneered at these complaints; his wife and two daughters came to our house regularly to buy wall decorations or new dresses. When I blew steam from underneath my lid and let it cloud my eyes for a second to keep me from looking at his hideous and imploring face, Abu Dawood would inevitably threaten to find out my secrets and announce them in the middle of the suq. After that, people would be talking about them until their voices grew hoarse.

The first time he threatened me, I thought about his words the whole evening and accidentally burned the lamb I was cooking. The next day, though, my fear was resolved: what could he tell about me that everyone didn't know? By the end of the week, when he was due to give me another pot full of jewels, he made the same threat. "Wallah? Really?" I said, letting my lid press down on my body in staged fear. "You're going to tell everyone Yama's majnoona, that I have no baba?"

He raised his eyebrows and glared intensely. "There's always a way to hurt someone." He slammed my lid down hard.

I turned away, kicking up as much dirt as I could manage without legs.

**Later that night,** I sat in Yama's lap while she stroked the side of my face; every now and then, she would pick off flakes of rust. "I can't believe how much you have aged, Tunjur," she said with a serenity she'd acquired from the comforts of protein and coal heating. "Everything's going well at the suq?"

"Yes, look at all I've brought home." I looked at the small sack of jewels in the corner; when I raised my eyes, I saw Yama looking at the same thing.

"I've never known people to be so generous," she said.

**I found Abu Farid** and Abu Dawood at the same booth, drinking coffee and eating dates. The two men hated each other, though they made polite conversation when necessary. Abu Farid looked down on Abu Dawood for eating the pork he supplied, but maybe he was just buttering Abu Dawood up again because he needed more money. If there was anything Abu Farid loved, it was spending all he had before it was even in his hands.

I jumped on Abu Dawood's booth as always, and he smiled when I demanded my payment. "Oh, sure, ya Tunjur," he said.

I lifted my lid, and because my eyes could not be open while the lid was off, I smelled the dung before I saw it. I slammed the lid down and smashed his hand. He cried out, but I made sure to crush his hand as much as I could, damaging every bone before I released it. "You better clean me out and give me my cut, sharmoot, or I'll tell everyone about your greed and pig-eating ways!" I shouted. My anger caused the dung to cook and fester even more.

He spit in my face and tried to force more dung under my lid, but I used my handles to press down hard, making the taste more intense. Abu Farid got up from his seat reluctantly and gently pushed Abu Dawood back. "Stop! She's learned her lesson. She won't get anything else. Just let her go home to her Yama."

And that's what I had to do because I was nearly gagging from the smell and taste. The only small relief I had as I clanked along was to let the shit spill out from my eyes.

**Yama was out the door** before I reached the house. Not only had she heard me clanking along the rocky ground, she smelled me well before that, believing one of the neighbours must have just gotten a whole slew of donkeys that had come down with a bad case of diarrhoea. "What's happened to you, ya Tunjur? You're full of shit!"

I confessed what I had been doing. She yelled at me for becoming a thief. "Ya haraam, ya haraam," she repeated over and over as if I didn't already know what I had been doing was wrong. I wanted her to clean me out before she punished me, but she picked me up and started running. I didn't have the courage to ask where we were going. I cried nearly the whole way, almost emptying myself out.

When my vision cleared, Yama and I were standing in front of Abu Dawood's house. She called for him to come out, and he did with his arms folded across his chest, looking smugly at the crowd that had gathered to see the next majnoona thing Yama would do. "What have you done to my daughter? Filled her with shit because of your sins, you pig-eating usurer?"

The crowd gasped at Yama's revelation and their eyes turned to Abu Dawood.

His face bleached to a pale yellow, and Yama took a handful of shit and flung it at his chest. She charged over to him and smeared what was left all over his face. He tried to push her away, but she slammed me against his head, taking him down in an instant.

Yama tore through the excited crowd to return to our home. She set me down and tears slipped from her eyes as she packed our things. She slung our bag of belongings over her shoulder and held me in the curve of her waist, my eyes pressed against her dress. "We will never see this village again."

# ASTURIAS

*Alison Braid*

*Alison Braid* is a Prague-based Canadian writer. Her work has appeared or is forthcoming in Train, Bad Nudes, The Puritan, Prairie Fire, CV2, The Maynard, Room, Barren, and Poetry Is Dead. Her poetry has received an honourable mention in Grain's 2018 Short Grain Contest and been shortlisted for CV2's 2018 Young Buck Poetry Prize.

## *A*STURIAS


Our campground pool a disturbance
of colour in the Green Belt while I'm
as I'll always be, clumsy in a red

one-piece. The bartender pours cider
from a great height to inject a flat
drink with effervescence, and in drunken

relaxation I pledge allegiance
to extended summer; to the sun,
a flat tennis ball; to magpies ducking

away in pairs. You ask what there is
to do:  pinhole camera, pinball, alcohol.
You're lonely in these puffed-up

days of summer. My own low-pressure
micro-climate prevails, wrings out
the pool's cobalt. Flash north storm

restores the deck to dampened
normality. A boy dives, orbits
something out of sight, surfaces

cold, colt-like. Obtained only water
to cup in his hands. I slump back
into myself, the lounge chair.

*A good day to fly*, says the boy's
mother, pointing to sky shot
through by absent airplanes.

# ON THE SIXTH DAY

*Deborah L Davitt*

**Deborah L Davitt** *was raised in Nevada but currently lives in Houston, Texas, with her husband and son. Her poetry has received Rhysling, Dwarf Star, and Pushcart nominations, and her short fiction has appeared in* InterGalactic Medicine Show, Compelling Science Fiction, Pseudopod, *and* Galaxy's Edge. *For more about her work, including her Edda-Earth novels and upcoming poetry collection,* The Gates of Never, *please see edda-earth.com.*

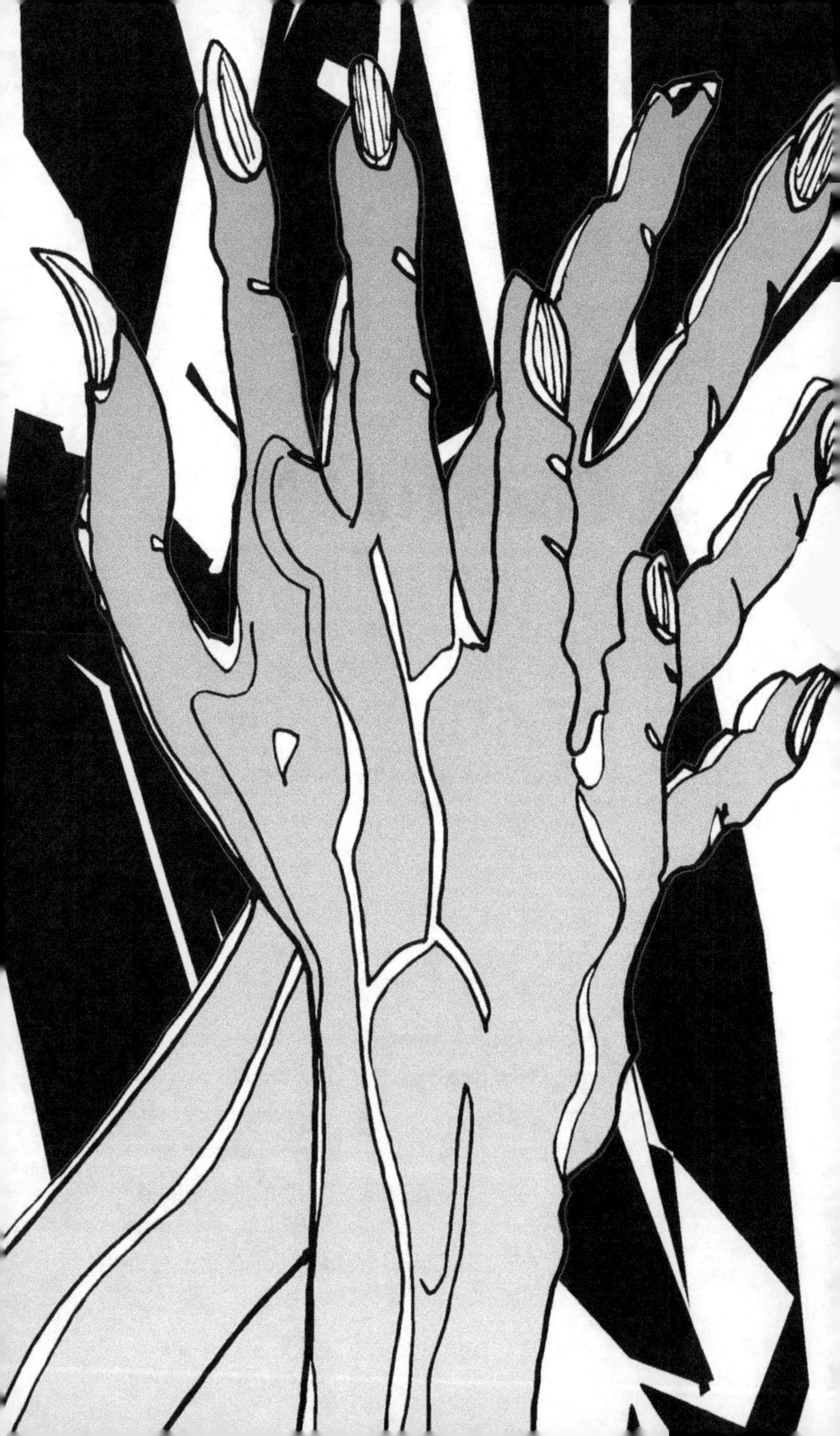

# ON THE SIXTH DAY

*Day Two*

**Liqui hunkered beside Phillipe warily.** Her hazmat suit reeked of two days' sweat. Their lab had been built at the bottom of an old missile silo, buried in bedrock so that, in case of emergency, the entire complex could be collapsed.

*In case of emergency.* She laughed nervously, earning a glare from Phillipe. "Something's funny?" His Québécois accent seemed harsher for the whisper.

Her laughter died. "We have to get to the director's office and push the button."

Phillipe hissed between his teeth. "You want us to commit suicide?" He shook his head. "We contact the CDC, the way the director should've—"

"She was infected—"

"She just didn't want her accreditation revoked." A snort. "We get to communications and radio out." Cell phones didn't work here, deep underground. "They'll get us out and contain the rest."

Liqui swallowed. *What if they decide to remote detonate?*

*Day Three*

**They'd planned to walk out** in full gear, passing their former co-workers in protective anonymity. But the infected somehow *knew* that Liqui and Phillipe weren't one of them. They'd watched, blank-eyed, lips moving in silent communion with the rest of their new collective intelligence. Then they'd converged.

The pair ran, feet pounding along the tiled corridors, and found disused labs in which to hide under equipment covered in plastic drapes.

The intercom crackled with the director's voice: "Phillipe Gangier and Liqui Huang are among the infected. The virus creates brain inflammation, sensitizing the amygdala to fear reactions, creating a sense of paranoia in those affected. Please use caution in approaching them, and be gentle with restraint procedures. They're our people, and they need our assistance." A pause. "Phillipe, Liqui, if you're hearing this … please come in. Let us help you."

Liqui swallowed. It sounded plausible. It would convince those not already infected, not already a part of the hivemind. It almost convinced her. "You don't suppose," she murmured, "that they might be correct? That we're the ones infected?"

Phillipe snorted. "We're the ones in hazmat gear. Not them."

Still, the thought nagged at her. *What if we're wrong?*

*Day Four*

**Locked in the communications room,** fists hammering at the door. Liqui's hands shook inside her blood-slicked hazmat gloves. They'd had to fight and risk compromising their gear. And when they'd arrived at the communications centre, she'd wanted to howl because every piece of gear had been smashed.

"I can fix this," Phillipe muttered, fumbling for tools. "Get a short message out."

"As if the director hasn't been sending out messages of her own, on the line in her office." Liqui slumped in a chair, head spinning from exhaustion.

"Sure, but we can't *get* to her office. Not through them." He nodded at the exit, vibrating from the impact of fists on the other side. "We need to barricade that."

She stood, shoving a nearby table towards the door. Everything felt far away. Four days with no sleep and little food. Constant anxiety and fear. *This is why soldiers have trouble with decision-making in combat. This is why orders are so important. I can't even think.* "I'm on it. Get the radio fixed, and we'll send a message out. Just the essentials. A virus breached containment. It changes brain structure the same way *Toxoplasma* does, except instead of decreasing the inhibitory effect of fear, it seems to join the infected into a hivemind ..." Liqui's voice trailed off as she noticed blood trickling from Phillipe's left sleeve. "You're hurt."

His dark face seemed paler than usual in the window of his hood. "A scratch," Phillipe replied. "If we use antiseptic, it might not be an issue. And if it is? You'll have a timeline for infection."

She doubted that his bravado fooled even himself.

*Day Six*

**"They've stopped banging at the door,"** Liqui whispered into the repaired radio. "It's been four hours since Phillipe fell unconscious."

Hunger gnawed her belly. "They know he's one of them. They're waiting for him to wake up." *When he'll attack me.*

She'd never felt so alone. Not even when she'd come to this country as a child, the only person in her class who couldn't speak English. At least all the strange faces then had still been human, understandable in flashes of pity or scorn. None of her classmates had been wrapped up in some insular inner world, lost in some ineffable communion. *Of course,* part of her mind nagged softly, *that could be paranoia. It's possible that you and Phillipe were the ones infected. That everyone else here is clean. That the voices on the radio to whom you've been talking are figments. That Phillipe's collapse is the virus's natural progression when left untreated for six days.*

She shook her head. "No, I have to trust myself. I have to trust the evidence of my own senses. If I don't, what else *can* I rely on?" Her voice seemed to fray into unreality at the edges.

Therein lay the problem. The human mind and senses were fallible. Memory was a reconstruction of actual events. Human senses lied. *What's real?*

Phillipe's eyes opened, and he sat up. "Liqui," he whispered with a smile. "It's not so bad." He held out a hand. "I feel good. Warm. Accepted. Part of something. Come with me. We'll walk out together."

Liqui swallowed, struggling. The words tempted her. A vision of reality: that there really *was* an infection. That giving in would mean never being alone again. Alone as she'd been as a child. Alone as she was now, the last person still free of the virus, surrounded by the hive.

Cold, clinical thoughts slid through her haze: *If this is real, then* this *must be contained. If it's not real, then nothing you say or do will have any effect. Choosing not to choose resolves nothing. So choose already.*

She closed her eyes against the yearning. "Detonate," she told her listeners as Phillipe took her hand. "If you're real, if you can hear me, detonate."

# BLACK MARKET

### Susan Pieters

***Susan Pieters*** raised three kids in East Van, and this story explains why she kept them home each night under lock and key. For more of Sue's stories, visit her eponymous website, susanpieters.com.

# $\mathcal{B}$LACK MARKET

**In East Van,** they sell the good stuff at midnight.

A black-hooded figure under movie-style lighting from a streetlamp gathers a crowd. Homeless people appear around him like rats emerging from the cracks of the sewer. They grovel at the edges of the light. "Please," say the wheedlers, the ones with no money and less hope.

The cloaked figure ignores them. Tonight he has more than uppers and downers. He has a special vial, kept warm in an inside pocket. It's marked 'Poet'.

A motorcycle pulls up, and a thick man in a leather jacket pulls out a large wad of cash. He wants the whole vial.

The hooded man laughs. "One dose at a time. Trust me." But he still demands all the cash. He tilts the biker's head back, bypasses the open mouth. He peels back one eyelid at a time, and with a dropper he puts dots of red liquid in each of the eyes. "Keep them closed until I tell you."

The others stand back. The light from the streetlamp falls to the wet, glistening pavement.

The man in the cloak counts his money slowly. "You can open them now."

The biker blinks, twice. Pulls his bushy hair away from his face. Turns around slowly.

The crowd is quiet, trying to see into his face, looking at his eyes to see if the blood is still there, the fresh, living poet's blood. It's illegal and rare. This is a first for them. But in the biker's eyes is no redness, no strangeness, no pink tinge to stain the tears that well up and flow down the cheeks.

One by one, the crowd turns away from those eyes. Those eyes *know* them. The biker now *sees* them. The biker sniffs like he can smell their need. Smell their pain.

God help him.

They forget about their own fix and the hunger in their veins. They step back, and like a spooked flock of crows, they leave en masse.

The hooded dealer laughs. Everyone but the biker has gone. "No more takers?" He puts the rest of the precious vial close to his chest to stay warm. "You seem to have ruined my business for the evening. But I'll make up for it tomorrow night. You'll be giving them something to think about. Such nightmares. They don't like seeing themselves."

The biker turns weeping eyes to the hooded figure. The streetlamp is a candle in the darkness, but it sheds nothing but more darkness. It lights up nothing good. The dealer's teeth click like fangs when he speaks, and he has snakeskin on his hands. Can he really see the hard-on the dealer gets from the money in his pocket?

"Oh my God," the biker says. "Oh my God."

# WALTZ FOR MY BROTHER

*Raluca Balasa*

**Raluca Balasa** *holds an MFA in Creative Writing from the University of Nevada, Reno. Her approach to writing is character-oriented, often dealing with love-hate relationships, antiheroes, and antagonists who make you agree with them. Her short work has appeared in* Andromeda Spaceways, Aurealis, Psychopomp, *and* Grimdark Magazine, *among others. Her poetry has appeared in* Fire Poetry. *When she's not writing, she can be found playing the piano or spilling things.*

# Waltz for My Brother

Looking at my brother in the cot,
spit trembling at the side of his mouth,
I know he will be a deviant.

He will feel wind in his veins. Voices
and footsteps will be harmony to
the melody in his cells. He will

want to join the pattering rain, the
bird calls, rug-beater, trickling fountain.
He will hear an equation that he

alone can solve. He'll be called names, told
that in this world, boys must abandon
colour and music for practical

ideas of avoiding pain. He will
be told to pay attention when he
wants to dream. He will be told to stay

awake. To stay, though no one wants him.
I don't want him, but I don't want him
to wither like me. We are coughs, stains.

*Allegro con fuoco* in a world
afraid of fire. So I gather
him and run. We will just keep moving,

'til our passing is as natural
as the changing seasons, and no one
thinks to ask of us any more than

they would ask
why summer
turns to fall.

# BIOPHILIA

## Margot Spronk

*Lapsed pilot, retired air traffic controller, cancer survivor, and graduate of Simon Fraser University's The Writers Studio. With all that behind her, **Margot Spronk** now has time to write. Currently she's working on an optimistic dystopian novel set in the far future. 'Rules of Salvage' appeared in* Pulp Literature *Issue 21. 'Biophilia' was the first runner-up for the 2018 Surrey International Writers' Conference Storyteller's Award, judged by Jack Whyte and Diana Gabaldon.*

# Biophilia

**A blowtorch hissed blue fire.** Between Casey's feet, the glowing tip of a leafy vine twitched as it turned to ash and drifted across his boots.

"Bindweed. It almost got you. Jeez, Casey."

The vine crackled as Mom scorched the plant back to where it emerged from the ground. With quick and practised swings of her spade, she dug up the dirt and charred the exposed white root-mat. This time the death wriggle was real, not the illusion of movement generated by compound carbon molecules breaking apart. After toasting the bare earth a few feet in every direction, she pounded an orange warning stake into the soil. "We're going to lose this area. Damn." She wiped the perspiration shine off her forehead with the back of her gloved hand.

Casey lifted each boot and examined the treads for root fragments. He splashed high-acid vinegar from the bottle he always carried. "Sorry, little plant," he whispered. Then much louder, "Sorry, Mom. I should've been paying more attention."

"We've come to the end of our border patrol anyway." She picked at the errant blonde hairs sweat had glued to her face.

"Let's go home. It's hot. I was hot before I set the ground on fire. My back aches. And … I'm getting contractions."

"No … Already?" Casey put out an arm to steady her. "You okay?"

"Yah." She waved him off. "Probably just Braxton Hicks. But after last time, I'm not taking any chances." She pressed the heels of her hands into her lower back, arching her belly forward, and groaned. "Did you know, before the Surge, parents could find out a baby's sex before birth?"

"Why would that matter, Mom?"

"People thought it was important." She twisted to take in the view.

They stood on a barren redoubt under the beating noontime sun, not a scrap of shade in sight. Below them, a smoky-green sea seeped between the tops of bent and broken buildings, but it wasn't water. Massive Douglas firs, red cedars, and broad-leaf maples were so densely packed that from a distance they appeared to flow. The actual ocean—a grey-blue reflecting the cerulean summer sky—curled around the forest-drowned city, snaking between the lower reaches of the mountain they stood upon and the thickly forested, violet-tinged mountains of the North Shore.

Mom sighed. "Still can't believe this really happened."

**Casey had been born** after the city drowned. He'd seen photographs, of course, but it was still difficult to imagine the undulating green vales below as a city. A city of thousands—no, millions. Towering high-rises, and small houses too; highways with speeding cars and trucks. And airplanes! Mom said it was never quiet. Horns and sirens, rumbling engines, people talking, and music everywhere.

How awful the panic must've been when the earthquakes came, followed by tsunami after tsunami. Then the Forest Surge gobbled up what little hadn't been pummelled to pieces and washed out to sea. Within a year, the city was sublimated under a verdant blanket of trees. The Forest Surge still pushed at the barriers that ringed the relatively unscathed mountaintop university. Ergo, the ever-vigilant Border Watch with their blue flame and vinegar.

They walked home along an asphalt path, past greenhouses set on cement slabs in the old University playing fields and the burnt-out remains of half-collapsed student residences. Casey torched a baby dandelion that had muscled through the tarmac and, further on, vinegar-dosed a thistle edging up beside an old building foundation. His mother shuffled behind him, cheeks ballooning, breath whistling between clenched teeth, determined to get home on her own. Far beyond noticing the wayward greenery.

**Casey's baby sister was born** a few hours later, three months early. After the last time, when Casey's would-be little brother died *in utero* and almost killed his mother, the midwife decided an emergency Cæsarean in the Urgent Care Centre's treatment room was the safest option, although she fretted at the field hospital conditions. Even though Casey wanted to stay with his mother to hold her hand and, quite frankly, to witness the gory miracle of birth, he wasn't allowed. He waited in the hallway outside, sitting on a plastic chair that flexed dangerously under his large frame, tensing with each muffled moan. Across from him, his father made notes on a tablet, tapping his heel to a rhythm only he could hear.

Finally, Casey was allowed to go into the delivery room. His mother looked pale against the bleached sheets, but she beamed when she introduced him to his swaddled sister. Alyssa. The baby gripped his forefinger with a tiny furry-knuckled hand and stared up at him with big blue eyes.

"I think she's so hairy because she's premature," Mom said. "It'll probably all fall out."

"How heavy is she?"

"Twelve pounds, six and a half ounces." She winced. "Did you know babies used to lose ten percent of their weight in their first week of life?"

He shook his head.

"Doesn't happen anymore. Your sister is already a very skilled and efficient nurser." She winced again.

**At three months,** Alyssa surpassed the ninetieth percentile for one-year-olds on the growth chart the midwife had posted in her office. By six months, Alyssa weighed thirty pounds, and her knuckles were still hairy.

What was normal anymore, anyway?

"She's growing faster than you did, Casey. There are species where females are larger than males. Wolf spiders." Mom shook her head. "That isn't a good example. The females will eat the smaller males if they're hungry enough. But blue whale females are larger than the males." She eyed her blimp-like son up and down. "Maybe that's not a good example either."

At six-foot-eight and two hundred and sixty-five pounds, Casey was a big four-year-old. In fact, he was the biggest person in the entire University population of five hundred and fifty-two. Largest because he was the oldest of the twenty-nine children born since the Forest Surge, although it appeared likely that the younger ones would eventually overtake him. He wasn't sure he wanted to be outgrown by his sister—whether or not she would one day eat him. Still, everything getting larger was just how things were. Radishes as big as softballs. Swiss chard as tall as he was. New Hampshire Reds lumbering about the chicken houses like crimson-plumed ostriches.

Pests, too, had exploded in size and corresponding ferocity. Aphids as big as peas—a new pea, which resembled a green Ping-Pong ball. Woolly caterpillars you could wear as a hat.

Not that you'd want to.

"You know, Casey, this isn't unprecedented. In the Pleistocene Epoch, there were many large mammals in North America. Beavers grew up to seven feet long and were as heavy as you are. Twenty-foot-long ground sloths weighed up to four tons. Mammoths stood thirteen feet at the shoulders, much taller than their modern elephant relatives."

Casey had never seen a real beaver or a sloth. Or an elephant, for that matter. He found a photographic reference book—*Earth's Animals in Pictures*, 2018 edition—in the Animal Biology section of the University library and brought it to show his mother. She'd been confined to home by the Board of Governors, where she busied herself spinning wool in the cosy living room of their two-bedroom apartment.

Mom palmed the spinning wheel to a stop and opened the book to a two-page panoramic spread of the African savannah. "Yes, Casey. This is what the animal kingdom was like before. We have no idea what's going on in the rest of the world now. Maybe it's like this but even more so." She pointed to the wildebeests and zebras drinking from a waterhole and then to the leopards lounging in a tree. "We don't even know what lives in the forest a few miles away. Clearly, it's an evolutionary process. But no one could've foreseen it moving this fast. Or in this direction. Before the Surge, many of these animals were on their way to extinction."

"The forest is noisy at night. Like a symphony of squawks and hoots and howls. Different tones and frequencies." Casey undulated his palm through the air. "I don't think anything is extinct."

"You shouldn't be outside at night. I don't want you in trouble with the Board of Governors too."

"What if I listen from the roof?"

"You can hear it from so far away? I'd love to do that. I could identify the species."

He nodded and picked up a set of carding paddles and a clump of washed smoky-green wool and began brushing the fibres straight.

"Do you like the colour?" Mom asked. "I made it from wild leaves." They sat in companionable silence, listening to the scritch of the paddles and the purring and clacking of the wheel, while Alyssa napped in her crib beside them.

Casey's mom was a palaeontologist, a professor at the University where they — and all the humanity left in the world, for all they knew — now lived. Most of the survivors of what she had since hypothesized was the Anthropocene Extinction Event were fellow academics or students who happened to be on the mountain when the earthquakes hit, forced to watch in horror as implacable forces pulverized the city below them. Once the Forest Surge started, they couldn't leave. And why would they? Everyone said there was nothing left down there.

Casey wasn't sure he believed it was the end of the Age of the Humans. Surely he was human, and Mom and Alyssa and all the people at the University too. She said it wasn't about individual humans but about dominance over the planet.

Oh.

"Sometimes I forget you are only four."

"Four and a half."

**Thursday afternoons Casey went to his father's lab** in the bio sciences building. Once Alyssa was one, she came too. Supposedly to learn science, but Casey spent most of the time preparing Father a week's worth of dinners and teaching Alyssa how to cook. He showed her how to cut up a chicken carcass, peel the vegetables, and simmer the stock in an iron crucible hung over a fire pit in the quadrangle, next to a concrete pond full of orange-and-black koi the size of dolphins. It was easier than doing it at home—Mom would make a sharp sucking sound every time he handed his sister a chef's knife.

Father was a small man … well, maybe more of an average-sized adult who wore threadbare band T-shirts and faux-leather jeans under his white lab coat and shaved his head to obscure his advancing baldness. A botanist, he was obsessed with finding the herbicide that would hold back the Forest Surge once and for all. He spent hours testing various compounds on his gridded control plots, while The White Stripes played on the sound system. His work was far too important for him to interrupt and attend community dinners. Still, Casey would've liked to do some hands-on experiments himself instead of just cooking and studying a copy of *Wild Plants of Coastal British Columbia* he'd found in Father's office.

After apportioning the soup into seven screw-topped glass jars and placing them on the top shelf of the specimen freezer, Casey quizzed Alyssa on the differences between an evergreen huckleberry and its inedible, noxious lookalike, the false azalea, until it was time to go home.

**Mom, Alyssa, and Casey lounged on lawn chairs** on the pebbled roof four stories up, a good half-mile away from the forest boundary. In the panorama before them, the sun's last rays gilded the ocean with pink and gold, brushing the distant mountains with a soft indigo. It was October. Maple trees lit the dark slopes closest to them with cheerful orange blotches. In places their already-bare branches interrupted the solid green of the conifers, making the forest seem almost penetrable.

Mom sat up abruptly in her lawn chair. "That sounded like a bull moose. But throatier. Honkier. Like a goose crossed with a moose."

High-pitched chirps, bass line hums, and the occasional hoot rounded out the forest's orchestral offerings. Casey found it soothing. He'd been dozing in his chair until his mother spoke.

Alyssa was a year and a third old now. Her flaxen head bent over a sketchpad, intent on capturing the subtle gradations of the sunset with broad strokes of paint and the liberal use of her still-downy fingers. The work was impressionistic.

Casey wasn't sure if that was intentional or due to a lack of skill. He made a mental note to give her some photographs to practise copying. Accuracy was foundational. After she'd mastered that, then she could exercise her imagination.

The next night was stormy, so Casey and Alyssa listened to the forest from under an overhang. The sounds were different. The susurration of wind-wracked trees, the thrumming of rain, and the crackle of thunder drowned out the animal noises — or perhaps quieted them. Lightning struck across the water. Roils of yellow and red flame and a black blacker than the sky boiled up from the forest.

"I'd like to paint that," Alyssa said.

They nibbled a ripened sheep's cheese Casey was testing out as they watched the fire rage up the hillside. Their mother wasn't with them. They hadn't seen her since the previous evening.

**By New Year's,** it was obvious where Mom had been. Her belly stuck out a mile. Father became more taciturn, avoiding his children even more assiduously. If the Board of Governors hadn't insisted he spend time with them, he would've locked his lab in their faces. He threw himself into his work, challenging himself by attacking the ferocious vanguards of the forest, Himalayan blackberry and *Convolvulus arvensis*, the aggressive bindweed whose vines and roots grew right in front of you. Casey wondered if Father had somehow conflated his helplessness in the face of Mom's ardour with his inability to quell the Forest Surge, thinking if he could contain one, he could contain the other.

If he was even that self-aware.

Spring turned the burnt patches across the water a pale green studded with charcoal spires. Later the green deepened, although it never became as dark as the surrounding forest. One morning, the meadows were splashed with vibrant yellow and purple.

"Wild flowers," Mom intoned from the lawn chair on the roof, where she sat knitting a long scarf out of smoky-green wool. "Hawksbeard? Fireweed? Oh! What's that black thing? It's moving."

Casey put down the ball of wool he was rolling off a skein Alyssa held out for him and handed Mom the binoculars. He already knew what it was. A black bear. He'd also seen elk and once a pack of wolves loping through the long grass.

"It's a bear," she whispered, leaning forward and peering through the lenses. "There always were a lot of bear around here. Even on campus. You know, we used to live with nature all around us. No barriers. Of course, we were the predators then." She sighed and was quiet for a moment. "He looks huge."

"He is. Factoring in the distance, I'd say he's at least twelve feet tall. Probably weighs more than a ton." Casey said.

"*Arctodus simus*—the short-faced bear—was about that big. They died out about ten thousand years ago." She turned toward her son. "I want to go out there. This is so amazing!"

"It can't be a real prehistoric bear, Mom. Besides, it's too dangerous, and you are way too pregnant." He handed her a glass of water. She needed to keep her fluids up, and she often forgot to drink. "And …" His voice faded off. "You're too small."

Mom sipped at the water. Her eyes got the faraway look they often had while she was processing big ideas. "You think this world isn't for me anymore."

Casey didn't say anything. He didn't tell her he and Alyssa had gone into the forest that morning. He didn't tell her that the wild green scent of it smelled like home.

"You're probably right, Casey. But I'd sure like to know what's happening and why."

**Before dawn, Casey and Alyssa** had scrambled over the twenty-foot concrete-and-steel Forest Surge barrier, crossed the sea of sterile salted mud named No-Green Land, fought through the tangle of bindweed and thorny blackberry infesting the forest margins, and slipped under the trees just as the sun was sending tentative shafts of light through the canopy. The pale glow, massive overarching grey trunks, and lush birdsong gave the space a cathedral quality.

In a solemn whisper, Alyssa named the plants and shrubs as they padded along a narrow deer trail. "Salal. Oregon grape —"

"Edible?"

"Yes. Salal berries are tastier than Oregon grape."

"When are they ripe?"

"Both in summer. Salal tastes sweeter, but Oregon grape has medicinal uses, too."

"Explain."

While Alyssa reeled off the health benefits, Casey listened to her, and to the forest sounds as they made their way deeper into its embrace: the soughing of the trees, the rustle of creatures in the underbrush, and the unwitting harmony of male sparrows and chickadees as they advertised for mates. He stopped where a pink sunbeam had gilded the tree trunks red and inhaled deeply. Musky, resinous. Clean.

"Were you listening, Casey?"

"Smell that, Alyssa. Smell the green."

**Barney was born by C-section in early April.** Eleven pounds, twelve ounces. Five and a half months gestation.

"Casey. Do you remember when Alyssa was born and I told you that babies used to lose ten percent of their body weight the first week?"

Casey nodded while he arranged the pillows behind his mother. Her hair, once a luxuriant blonde she'd passed on to her children, had with this pregnancy faded to grey. Her face, once a sun-kissed tan, had paled to a sallow yellow.

"I think it's the mothers who lose the weight now. It's something you must watch for. Make sure the moms get as much nutrition as they can. Promise me."

"I promise, Mom."

She floated back to sleep. Casey took Barney out of the hospital room crib and fed him sheep's milk from a bottle while walking around the Urgent Care Centre lobby. He couldn't sit in the plastic chairs anymore.

At a lanky seven-foot-seven and three hundred and ten pounds, Casey didn't fit in any of the furniture. He'd also hit puberty. His voice kept flipping an octave, he felt stinky-sweaty all the time, and he was beginning to get what drove his mother to seek out his father.

Not that he had anyone in mind.

There was a five-year-old who lived down the hall. Like Alyssa, a silky down covered Lizzie's whole body — what he could see of it. She was almost seven feet of solid muscle.

"Casey."

"Yes, Mom?" He walked back into her room, bouncing Barney, hoping he'd burp.

Her breath rasped like fizzing bubbles. "I've been thinking a lot about what's coming. I want you to know that I think you — and your sister — are doing everything right. Everything according to Gaia's plan."

Casey rolled his eyes.

"No. Don't scoff." She smiled, a small, self-deprecating half smile. "This is my area of expertise."

"Okay." He rubbed Barney's back in slow circles.

"I think this is all intentional. Evolution doesn't make big changes in a generation. Not ones that stick, anyway. I don't know who, and I don't know how. Maybe if one thing changes, it reverberates through every species." She took a wheezy breath. "We know it worked that way in the other direction. As humans, we started many ecosystems on the road to total collapse by changing just one little thing. Introducing an invasive, or eliminating a pest. Even if I don't know who, or how . . . I think I know why. *Homo gigantus*—"

Casey guffawed. She laughed too, although it ended in a cough.

"It's a working title. Females will be larger than males. That will hold toxic masculinity in check. And you won't live long, my love. Twenty years, maybe. Not long enough to rebuild civilization. I'm sorry. But it's obvious your lives have been accelerated. You'll be sexually mature at six."

Casey looked away; heat prickled his cheeks and the tips of his ears.

"She—if it is Gaia—has compensated you handsomely, though. You're brilliant, caring, and competent. You might yet outsmart her. I'm very proud that you are my son, and I'm glad I had a part in bringing *Homo gigantus* into being."

Mom smiled, her eyes crinkling. Casey perched on the edge of her bed without resting his weight but still sank into the warmth of her expression, gathering up all the love she projected and reflecting it back to her tenfold.

Barney burped, and they both laughed. She stretched out a tremulous hand and stroked the baby's downy cheek.

Sometime in the night, Mom died. They buried her just west of the greenhouses, where she could watch the sheep get big and woolly in their pens and the sun set over the forest she never got to visit. The Chancellor spoke of her many academic achievements, her Border Watch service, and her knitting. In the audience, all the children held onto their tiny mothers' hands. Alyssa gripped Casey's hand with steely fingers. With Barney cradled in his other arm, he couldn't blot the tears sliding down the slant of his cheekbones and dripping into his ears. The hard lump in his throat wouldn't swallow away. The adults droned on and on, a palpable fear spalling off their voices as they reminisced about his mom. Afterwards, Father sprayed his latest herbicide over her grave.

Casey sort of understood. Still, it felt like repudiation.

The Board wanted the three children to live with their father, but they stayed in Mom's apartment. Casey had been looking after everything anyway.

Father was relieved.


**In June of that summer,** Lizzie's mom died in childbirth. The funeral drew almost all six hundred members of the University community to the cemetery by the greenhouses. Casey stood at the back, nestling a sleeping Barney against his shoulder, again holding Alyssa's hand. Over the adults' heads, he could easily see the Chancellor waiting to speak beside the newly dug grave, but his attention was inexorably drawn to his mother's resting place, a barren mound topped with a concrete slab a dozen yards off to the left. The Chancellor, backlit by the late afternoon sun, cleared his throat. The crowd's murmuring stopped.

"Thank you all for coming to honour the life of Dr Sil—"

Lizzie ploughed through the crowd and thumped down beside her mother's grave, knees sinking in the loose dirt. She spread a lush bouquet of yellow hawksbeard, purple foxglove, and salal down on the freshly turned soil then stood up—eyes glittering—and ran behind the greenhouses, disappearing.

The Chancellor's voice stalled. He twisted the paper copy of his speech in his hands. Those standing closest to the grave stepped back, and those in back pushed forward, wanting to see what happened. A disturbed mutter rose.

An adult Border Guard dosed the ad hoc funeral spray with a whole bottle of vinegar. Another Guard joined him, sweeping a blazing blowtorch across the grave. Blue flames crackled, blistering the delicate flowers and fronds into black wisps of ash.

The Chancellor resumed his speech, but Casey didn't stay to listen. He went looking for Lizzie. She wasn't home. She wasn't at the koi pond or in the library. She wasn't anywhere at the University as far as he could tell. When he caught up with her the next day, the leaves and needles stuck in her hair told the story of where she'd been.

He put his arms around her, and she sobbed against his shoulder while he stroked her agitated fur flat through her shirt. The lump lodged in his throat since his mom's death enlarged, and with it, the first stirring of a sense that it was up to him to stand up for all the children. He was the oldest. He'd always been a good kid. The adults should listen to him.

A few days later, Father announced he would run for Chancellor in the September elections. '*Homo sapiens* forever' would be his campaign slogan. It had already caught on. One morning, on his way to Father's lab, Casey found it spray-painted in fluorescent yellow on the pitted concrete walls of the bio sciences building. On his way home, smears of leafy green and what he hoped was dirt had obliterated the word *sapiens*.

Then another mother died. Her four-year-old son—Stanley— laid down an even larger, more elaborate bunch of wild flowers on her grave and ran off like Lizzie had. Two Border Guards standing by with blowtorches quickly turned the floral arrangement into a smoking, acrid pile of charcoal.

Casey stood up at a Senate meeting called to decide how to deal with Stanley and Lizzie's violation of University rules. He explained they were just expressing their loss in a naturally rebellious manner. They were the new equivalent of teenagers, after all.

The Board members scoffed. These were four- and five-year-olds, who — while they might be large — were still just … children. The Chancellor thanked Casey for his input, rapped his gavel to end discussion, and adjourned the public meeting into a closed session. As the gallery cleared and the spectators shuffled out the door, Casey overheard someone say they were going to talk about the abysmal state of birth control research.

Birth control. He might have been just … a child, but he knew what that meant.

The Board ruled to ground the flower bringers.

When Casey told her, Lizzie laughed, a deep stuttered roar like that of a coughing lion. He explained what his mother said about *Homo gigantus.* How the world had been before the Anthropocene Extinction Event, and why adults were afraid of anything green.

She popped a blackberry in her mouth and shrugged, the fur on her shoulders rippling silver over her trapezius muscles. "There's nothing to be afraid of," she said.

Lizzie and a gang of kids moved into a derelict residence and stole food from the dining hall and greenhouses. They stopped going out with the Border Patrol.

Weeds popped up along University paths. Thistle. Dandelion. Butterflies with a ten-inch wingspan and bees the size of teacups followed, in search of pollen and nectar. Casey crouched down beside a sunny yellow dandelion, plucked one of the flower's spear-shaped leaves, and chewed off a bit. Bitter and green. Wild. His body throbbed with longing.

Why hadn't his mother spoken to the Senate?

Or … had she? They probably thought she was crazy. They thought he was just a precocious child. He could talk his head off, and it would change nothing.

He was afraid. Afraid for the adults, the last vestiges of *Homo sapiens*, afraid their stubborn clinging to the past would end up killing them. Afraid their fear of the new would end up killing their children, *Homo gigantus*.

And the forest's call was green and insistent.

Casey rubbed his itchy beard. It was growing in thick and fast. He was six years old. Alyssa had just turned two. Barney was three months and starting to walk and talk. He hoped Lizzie and the other kids would come, but either way, it was time to go down into the forest.

He devised a packing list.

1. *Wild Plants of Coastal British Columbia.*
2. *Earth's Animals in Pictures*, 2018 edition.
3. A wheel of sheep's cheese from his latest batch.
4. Mom's smoky-green wool and the sweaters and scarves she'd knitted.
5. Barney's diapers — although he wouldn't need those much longer.
6. Alyssa's paints.

But not his bottle of vinegar, or his blowtorch. He'd leave those at Father's door.

# WHITE RABBIT

*Deepthi Atukorala*

*Deepthi Atukorala* was an avid reader who recently lifted her head up from other people's stories to start writing her own. She lives in Vancouver and writes poetry, fiction, and non-fiction. She is a graduate of The Writer's Studio at Simon Fraser University and is published in the anthology Emerge. Her short story 'White Rabbit' was the second runner-up for the 2018 Surrey International Writers' Conference Storyteller's Award, judged by Jack Whyte and Diana Gabaldon. Connect with Deepthi on Twitter @DeepthiAtu.

# $\mathcal{W}$HITE RABBIT

**Papa holds my hand tight** because he doesn't want to lose me in the crowd. When we walk in to the Great Books hall from the hot-hot parking lot, the cold air-conditioned whoosh of new-book smell hugs us, and I can't stop smiling. I am wearing my ladybirds skirt especially for today.

Inside, big lights shine on red, blue, green, yellow, brown, orange mountains of books with English, Sinhala, and Tamil letters. My heart thumps all the way to my ears. Even if I am just learning how to put letters together to make words, I love them all. Everywhere, kids and mothers and fathers are touching books, flipping books, and standing in long line-ups with piles of books in their arms. I am trying to see around all the busyness to spot the Ladybird stall.

"Stop jumping, Shani," Papa says, pulling at my hand. It's good when my hand is in his warm hand.

Tikiri, who is not two yet and can only walk wobbly, tries to wiggle down from Mama's arms, but Mama says, "No you can't, sweetie. It's too busy here."

I know which way to go. Far back down the tunnel of stalls, ladybirds are climbing a stall roof, and I am sure kids are buying up all the good Ladybird books right now. I want to run there, and Papa is too slow.

"Look, Papa, Ladybird is so far away. We have to hurry, or all the good books will be gone." I have to shout so Papa can hear.

Mama says, "You take Shani. I'll follow."

I skip around pant legs, sari bottoms, tall skirts, and short skirts to get there quick. Papa is walking fast too, until suddenly he squeezes my hand and stops, making people bump into us.

"Papa, come on, let's go." I try to pull him, but I can't. He is staring to the side, and I am too short to see where.

"Papa!" But he is a statue.

I dodge a pant leg, peep over a stack of books, and I see her—Siriya.

She is wearing a yellow dress and stands with a bundle of books in her arms, looking tiny and very-very pretty, same like when she first visited us. But her long plait is short, only long enough for the bushy end to sweep the top book.

I shout, "Siriya! Siriya!"

But Papa pulls me up around my tummy to his chest like I am a baby and puts his hand over my mouth. I look over his shoulder. Siriya stares at us. I try to wave but my hand is stuck, and then I can't see her anymore.

Papa says, "We have to go."

Mama asks, "Why?"

Papa just says, "We have to go."

I pull Papa's hand from my mouth and say, "Siriya is here, Mama, but Papa didn't let me talk to her."

Mama holds Tikiri flat in her arms like a baby and starts walking fast to the door. "Shani, we have to go."

I wiggle out of Papa's arms. I want to cry and say, "You promised Ladybird books," but Papa's got the sneezy Duchess-in-the-pepper-cloud face that he gets when he is upset. But I am more scared because Mama has her quiet face. If Mama gets quiet, she stops talking to everyone for long days. So I don't fuss.

Around us, people walk slow with their heads already in the stories they carry in overflowing boxes and bags. We are the only people rushing away with empty arms. I can't see my way because of the tears, but I try hard not to cry.

Only Tikiri is talking. "We have to go. We have to go," she says in a sing-song voice.

In the car even Tikiri is quiet. She hugs White Rabbit and stares out the window. White Rabbit stares at me with its red eyes. Papa brought him for Tikiri when she was still a new baby and didn't know about *Alice in Wonderland*. It's grey now, and its red waistcoat is a kind of orange. Mama brought lots of other rabbits and bunnies to take this one's place, but Tikiri only wanted her first one. Just like the big Alice book Papa brought for me at the same time is only my second favourite. My favourite Alice is my first one, the one with the bumped-out White Rabbit on the cover.

Siriya loved that book too, both times: the first time, and the time she was sick.

That first time, she sat on my bed, running her hand up and down the cover to feel White Rabbit, and said, "I like bunnies."

"That's not a bunny. That is White Rabbit." I took the book and turned the pages to show her. "See? He is running, looking at his pocket watch. See Alice following him? He went into a rabbit hole, and Alice fell a long way, into a very strange place where people were very odd."

Siriya is Great-uncle Jaya's daughter. She probably didn't know about Alice because she was poor. It was Mama who told us she was poor.

We were having dinner, and she told Papa, "Hon, Great-uncle Jaya came today to ask if you would have a job for his daughter. She's just finished high school, and they are really poor. Please, do what you can to help them."

Papa made a face. "Oh, I don't know how these village girls will fit in our office. Why don't you ask him to bring her over?"

Great-uncle Jaya and Siriya came to have Sunday lunch with us. Because Papa had lunch at home only on Sundays, we had chicken biryani, hard-boiled eggs to decorate the rice, mint sambol to settle the tummy, and cucumber salad to cool us. Dessert was caramel pudding, because it was Papa's favourite.

Siriya was the most beautiful girl I had seen, even if she was from the village. She had sparkly big eyes, a smiley mouth, and shiny black hair in a plait that fell all the way to her knees. When we sat down for lunch, Siriya tossed her plait over the chair back and its bushy end swept the floor.

Papa lifted me to the chair next to Siriya.

He said, "I married a girl with hair just like that."

I didn't understand until Mama laughed, smoothed her short straight hair, and said, "Yes. Until children come along, one can have long hair."

"You used to keep yours loose down your back," Papa said. He was looking at Siriya, but Siriya was looking at her hands on her lap.

Great-uncle Jaya cleared his throat and asked Mama, "How long have you two been married now, Daughter?"

"Too long, Uncle," Mama said, and Great-uncle Jaya laughed, but he was the only one.

After lunch, because Siriya became my friend, I took her to my room. Her big eyes grew bigger and rounder when she saw my pink-and-white room and all my books.

"What is your favourite story, Shani?" Siriya asked, peeping at my book rack.

"My favourite story is the story of me."

"Story of you?"

"Didn't your Mama tell you the story of you?" I had thought all the children knew their story.

Siriya shook her head.

"Well, do you want to hear mine?"

When I was little I used to talk a lot, because I hadn't figured out that sometimes the things I said could make Mama quiet. So even before Siriya said yes, I was telling her the story.

"Before I came, Mama was very sad because she didn't have a baby. For ten years she went to all the Hindu temples, Saint Anthony's church, Saint Jude's church, to ask all the gods and saints for a baby. Then one day, the gods gave her a test. They sent a girl who had been chased from her home by her family. Imagine that! I don't know what I'd do. Mama made everything right for this girl, even if it broke Mama's heart. When the gods saw this, they made her wish come true and gave me to her. She says it was the hardest thing she ever did, but I was worth it."

Siriya sat next to me on the bed and touched my hand, and I rushed on, "Mama had this room all set up with white furniture and white curtains and waited with a can of pink paint and a can of blue paint. When I was born, she painted the room pink with her own hands."

"This is such a beautiful room," Siriya said, looking around the room. But she had stopped smiling.

Great-uncle Jaya and Siriya left after tea, and I was sad. I asked Mama if I could have a sister like Siriya who could read books to me, but Mama just laughed. So I started praying to the gods for a sister.

Later Papa told Mama that he had a job for Siriya in his company and to let Great-uncle Jaya know. I asked Mama and Papa if Siriya could come and live with us and go to work.

Papa said, "Well, sure she can, sweetie. It will be good for both of you."

But Mama said, "No, we are fine. Let her come to work from her home."

After that I forgot about Siriya.

One morning when I woke up, there was a scruffy brown suitcase by my chest of drawers. When I went looking for Mama, Siriya was sitting at the kitchen table, having tea and biscuits.

"Siriya!" I yelled, and hugged her. She hugged me back, and I thought the gods had listened to my prayers.

But it wasn't like I thought it would be. Siriya had stopped being fun, probably because she was sick. Mostly, she slept, and when she was up, she didn't talk or smile like last time. She was so slow and didn't look too pretty anymore. When Mama told her, she sewed little white and yellow tops. I stopped praying because this was a different sister than the one I wanted. At night she sniffled and sniffled and her eyes were always red.

Sometimes Mama talked to Siriya in a low voice. "You can tell me, I won't tell your parents." But Siriya just looked down and shook her head, and tears fell from her eyelashes like the monsoons.

When Mama wasn't home, Papa sometimes tried to help Siriya. He needed peace and quiet to talk to her, so he sat me in his chair and let me use the TV remote. It was a secret, because if Mama found out she'd be really mad that I watched TV by myself. I think Papa was good at cheering Siriya, because later she would come and sit with me, plaiting her long hair and laughing at the cartoons.

The gods had finally heard my prayers from before, because Mama started changing the sewing room into a baby room. She bought baby furniture and two cans of paint — pink and blue.

She said, "We don't know if it will be a brother or a sister, but either would be wonderful."

Siriya stayed a long time with us. Sometimes Mama had to comb her long hair. Once she asked if Mama cut her hair when she was pregnant with me, and Mama put down the brush and left the room. Siriya started to cry, so I said I would comb her hair, but she didn't even say thank you at the end. So I wasn't sorry when she went away. Besides, I was getting my baby sister or brother.

One day Mama painted the baby room pink, and Mama and Papa brought brand-new Tikiri home. She was like a little kitten at first. Then in a few days she became pretty, with big round eyes and a big smile. She loved being tickled, and laughed and laughed, making us all laugh too. Everything became happy.

That's when Papa gave her the White Rabbit. As soon as I saw it with the red waistcoat, I knew it was him — not a bunny, not any old rabbit. It was Alice's White Rabbit, and that's what I call it. But Tikiri calls it Wabbit because she is too little to know Alice.

"Wee have to gooo." Tikiri has laid White Rabbit flat on her lap like a baby and is singing to it. She takes her blankie and covers him like she is putting him to sleep. And suddenly

I remember. I saw that White Rabbit before — lying in Siriya's brown suitcase.

I don't know why I didn't remember this before.

It was the day she was leaving, and in that mad rush, she took the folded clothes from her dresser drawer and opened her suitcase and dumped them all in. I saw the rabbit in the bag just before the clothes covered it.

I wanted to say, "Oh, is that White Rabbit?" but Siriya had already closed the suitcase and was holding her side, groaning. Then she started to cry. Mama came in and took the suitcase and took Siriya's arm to help her out to the car.

What if the one Siriya had was Tikiri's rabbit?

Then, somehow, I know it is the same rabbit — the same floppy ears, the same red eyes, the same red waistcoat.

Did Siriya give the rabbit to Papa? Why didn't she come to see Tikiri herself and give it? Why did she give it to Papa and not Mama? Where did she meet Papa and not us?

My tummy starts to hurt.

"Mama, my tummy hurts," I say. I bend over, and it is hard to breathe.

"I'll give you some gripe water when we get home," Mama says without looking back.

"Mama!" I am hurting, and she isn't looking.

Instead, she turns to Papa. "I can't do this anymore."

Papa just drives.

"Did you hear me?" Mama's usually soft voice is sharp, like a knife on a coconut. "I can't do this anymore. Fifteen years is enough."

I pull White Rabbit from Tikiri's hands and throw it to the front.

"I hate that rabbit!" I yell, and kick Papa's seat.

"I hate it, I hate it, I hate it."

Tikiri starts to cry. "Mama … Wabbit …" Her too-big eyes are all watery and red, but I don't care, and Mama doesn't either. She is busy glaring at Papa.

White Rabbit flops on the dashboard, one arm dangling over, staring at Papa with his red-red eyes.

Papa is driving like Rabbit isn't staring, Mama isn't glaring, Tikiri isn't crying, and I am not kicking his seat and yelling.

But I know he can't pretend for long.

"I hate you," I tell him. And I do.

# THE BUMBLEBEE FLASH FICTION CONTEST

# THE BUMBLEBEE FLASH FICTION CONTEST

**We always** start off the new year with the Bumblebee Flash Fiction Contest. It's a bit strange, perhaps, given most bumblebees are slumbering soundly at that time of year; however, during the summer, bumblebees are at their best, so we publish our winners in the summer issue. This year, the undisputed champion of flash fiction, Bob Thurber, issued the following proclamation:

*It was a tight race and a close call with all the pieces selected as finalists, but in the end I found this well-blended, post-modernized, traditional folk tale sparkled brighter than the rest.*

We are of a hive mind and can finally share 'Wife Giver', by Josephine Greenland, with readers here in Issue 23!

*Bumblebee Flash Fiction Contest 2019 Short List:*
**Andrew Owen Dugas** for 'Throwdown'
**Jess Simms** for 'The Werewolf at the Farmer's Market'
**Josephine Greenland** for 'Wife Giver'
**Kate Felix** for 'Class Party'
**KT Wagner** for 'Meals Not Eaten'
**Nancy Ludmerer** for 'Summation'
**Nancy Ludmerer** for 'Complicity'
**Ron Lavalette** for 'Crickets'
**Soramimi Hanarejima** for 'The Sublime is Difficult to Replifake'
**Zoë Johnson** for 'Inherited Love of Unexplainable Things'

The short list was incredibly strong this year, and even though there is no runner-up prize, the editors and Bob all agree that Honourable Mention goes to 'Inherited Love of Unexplainable Things' by Zoë Johnson.

Many thanks to our contestants with their sharp submissions of flash fiction. Your love of the craft keeps the contest going strong — we'll be waiting to hear from you in 2020.

*Josephine Greenland is a Swedish-British writer from Eskilstuna, Sweden. She holds an MA in creative writing from the University of Birmingham and a BA in English from the University of Exeter. Her short stories and poetry have been published in eight different magazines online and in print, including* Dream Catcher, Litro, *and* Literary Yard. *In 2018 she won the Fantastic Female Fables Competition by Fantastic Books Publishing and was a runner-up in the 2018 Summer Solstice Competition by Wild Words. She has also been highly commended in two competitions. In 2017 she received the Young Writer's Bursary from the Budleigh Salterton Literary Festival. When she isn't writing, she enjoys playing her violin and hiking with her family. You can follow Josephine on Twitter @greenland_jm.*

*Zoë Johnson is an emerging queer transgender writer living in the mid-Michigan area. They are Anishinaabe, of the Sault Ste Marie Tribe of Chippewa Indians. Currently they are a graduate student in the creative writing MFA program at the Institute of American Indian Arts. Work of theirs has been published by the* Sonora Review Online *and is forthcoming in the second edition of* Trans Bodies, Trans Selves *from Oxford University Press. This story was the editors' choice honourable mention in the 2019 Bumblebee Flash Fiction Contest.*

# WIFE GIVER

BY JOSEPHINE GREENLAND

**I guess I agreed to this.** Skin to cellulose, flesh to fibre. Blood to latex, bones to roots. Woman took man, man must return woman to earth.

It's like going to sleep, except the sheet you pull over your head is soil.

So they say — those men who will walk, sit, spit, and piss on the ground to be my bed.

In time they will forget me. There are always other women. My suitors will approach them with their promises in one hand and their cock in the other, our betrothal shoved into the bushes.

At first there were one hundred. I narrowed it down to seven. The fools all proposed on the same day. What did they think this was, a game of first come, first served?

Cause no friction, you said. Cause no jealousy. So I took all seven. Treat everyone as equal, isn't that the Akha way? Wasn't that your way, Papa, with those women who weren't my mama?

I guess you would shrug. Like father, like son. All a daughter needs is the power between her legs and enough willpower not to abuse it.

Did you know that mama still sleeps facing the door? All these years, she's stayed off your side of the bed, just in case you'd get it into your head (or manhood) to return. Whenever I've told her this, she looks away, holding on to the little dignity you haven't robbed her of already.

Perhaps in your mind, I want to be buried alive, tucked away in my sins. You need me to want it, don't you? Woman cannot claim man.

It's stuffy down here. You failed to mention that. Earth squeezes the oxygen out of my lungs and crawls into my mouth — iron and minerals on my tongue. Minty grass in my nostrils. Crumbling black on my pupil.

I rise and stand.

The word 'big' loses its value when you're a plant. Everything is *up*, everything is *more*. It makes me dizzy. My stalk body bends at the top, my bulb head tucks in its chin. If only I had arms and legs, to tuck the dizziness in, to help me balance.

Pins and needles prick the absence where my limbs should be. I've heard of phantom pains. One of my seven lost a leg to gangrene. An army of ants, he said, eating their way through the length of him. The sting of their bites festered long after the limb was gone.

My limbs are in here somewhere. Embedded in the fibres, flexing fingers and toes.

Pity they will never see daylight again.

For here you come in all your splendour. Man, master of all things. Knife at the ready, although harvest is two moons away.

But that was always your way, wasn't it? Plucking things before their time?

Call me by my name, before your mind is too slurred to think it. See the woman inside the flower's milky sap, before you cut it and dry it and smoke it. Burials of the body are commas, burials of the soul full stops.

Papaver somniferum. P for *papa*. Those stolen moments we had before you cut our bond in two … A father picking scraps of chicken meat from his daughter's teeth with a tiger tooth. Moments within moments that will soon be lost to you, permanently.

Perhaps this will hurt more than a little. Our bond is cut but our blood remains the same. The choices of one affect the choices of the other.

We must both see this through to the end.

*Once, there was a young girl so beautiful she had many suitors. Of all these, seven men impressed her. One day, all seven came to ask for her hand in marriage. The girl did not want to choose one from among them for fear of making the others sad and jealous. She therefore decided to make love to all seven men, even though she knew that it would surely cause her death. When she could endure it no more she asked for death and to be reincarnated as a beautiful flower. Before dying, she told her relatives to take good care of her grave, on which the flower would grow up from her heart. She said that whoever tasted the flower's sap would like it and want more but that it would bear both good and evil.*

*~ The Akha* legend on the origin of opium*

* The Akha are a hill tribe in northern Thailand.

# Inherited Love of Unexplainable Things

by Zoë Johnson

Detroit — 1977

**When you were little,** your daddy was always telling you that the most precious things in this world were the things you couldn't explain.

Mysteries, he would say, are what make life worth living. The things that don't follow rules, that defy common sense — things with magic at the core of them. Things like Black folk's hair and the grace of God. Things like you and your sister and your mama.

He would always say the last one with that sly wide grin of his, and your mama would always smack his arm but you could always tell she was smiling.

Your daddy is the one who teaches you to look for the small and miraculous things and after a while, you feel you've gotten pretty good at noticing them.

The way Miss Minnie bakes pies in the church basement and you can smell them all the way through service. The way Imani, without fail, arrives at school every Monday with a brand-new rhyme to jump rope to. The way lines of skin appear when a girl does her hair up in cornrows—like some secret language of Black beauty written out before you.

Maybe it was your daddy's influence, or maybe your inherited love of unexplainable things, or maybe it's just a mystery in and of itself that you become addicted to the way it makes you feel when a pretty girl lays eyes on you.

It isn't until you're sixteen and a girl calls you 'baby' with her lips pressed to your ear that the idea of *you* being one of the world's unexplainable and magical things occurs to you. It is a current of electricity passing through you, and you spend the next handful of years wrapping fingers around every exposed wire you can find.

By the time you live near Palmer Park, a different girl is calling you 'baby', and you think you love her but you don't dare admit it out loud before she does. You wear your hair in an afro that settles like a cloud around your face. You dress in men's shirts and walk the streets of Palmer Park with your chin up.

You read lots of books about black liberation that you wish were queerer and lots of books about queer liberation that you wish were blacker.

The first time you perform in drag, it's the closest to being a mystery you might have ever been. You feel like a thing made of nothing but glitter and smoke and the sound of your daddy's voice when he would say *'things that got magic in 'em'*.

Masculinity sure does feel like a kind of magic when it settles across your shoulders, at your hips, your jawline.

You don't think you feel like a boy. But sometimes being a girl clings—a shirt fitting too tight around your biceps or too loose around your ribs. But your daddy raised you on the belief of miracles being miraculous because they didn't always make sense. And you are nothing if not your daddy's child.

Maybe that's just part of the magic of you: the confusion.

On a Saturday morning in May your lover murmurs into your collarbone that you remind her of a plant that leans toward sunlight, with roots always stationary while the rest of you will twist and turn in whichever direction is nourishing you.

You take her hand and kiss her hair and think maybe tomorrow you'll wear your new vest and tell her you love her out loud.

# PULP Literature

Four awards for genre-busting fiction and poetry

## The Bumblebee Flash Fiction Contest

Deadline: 15 February
Prize: $300

## The Magpie Award for Poetry

Deadline: 15 April
First Prize: $500

## The Hummingbird Flash Fiction Prize

Deadline: 15 June
Prize: $300

## The Raven Short Story Contest

Deadline: 15 October
Prize: $300

For more information visit: pulpliterature.com/contests

Short stories, poetry, and comics you can't put down.

# WALL STREET AT NIGHT

## Lola Ridge and
## Chaille Stovall

**Lola Ridge** (1873–1941) was born in Ireland, grew up in the Antipodes, and immigrated to the US in her thirties. An influential editor of avant-garde, feminist, and Marxist publications, she was an advocate for women's rights, gay rights, and the rights of immigrants. In 1927, she was arrested while protesting the execution of Italian immigrant anarchists who were convicted through a controversial trial. Her awards included a Guggenheim Fellowship in 1935 and the Shelley Memorial Award in 1936.

**Chaille Stovall** is an illustrator from Miami, Florida. Inspired by storybooks and illuminated texts, Chaille Stovall's comic-book adaptations of literature try to capture the surreal experience of reading poetry and prose.

WALL STREET

AT NIGHT

Long vast shapes... 
cooled and flushed through with darkness...

Lidless windows

Glazed with a flashy luster

From some little pert café chirping up like a sparrow.

And down

among iron guts

Piled silver

Throwing gray spatter of light...
pale without heat...

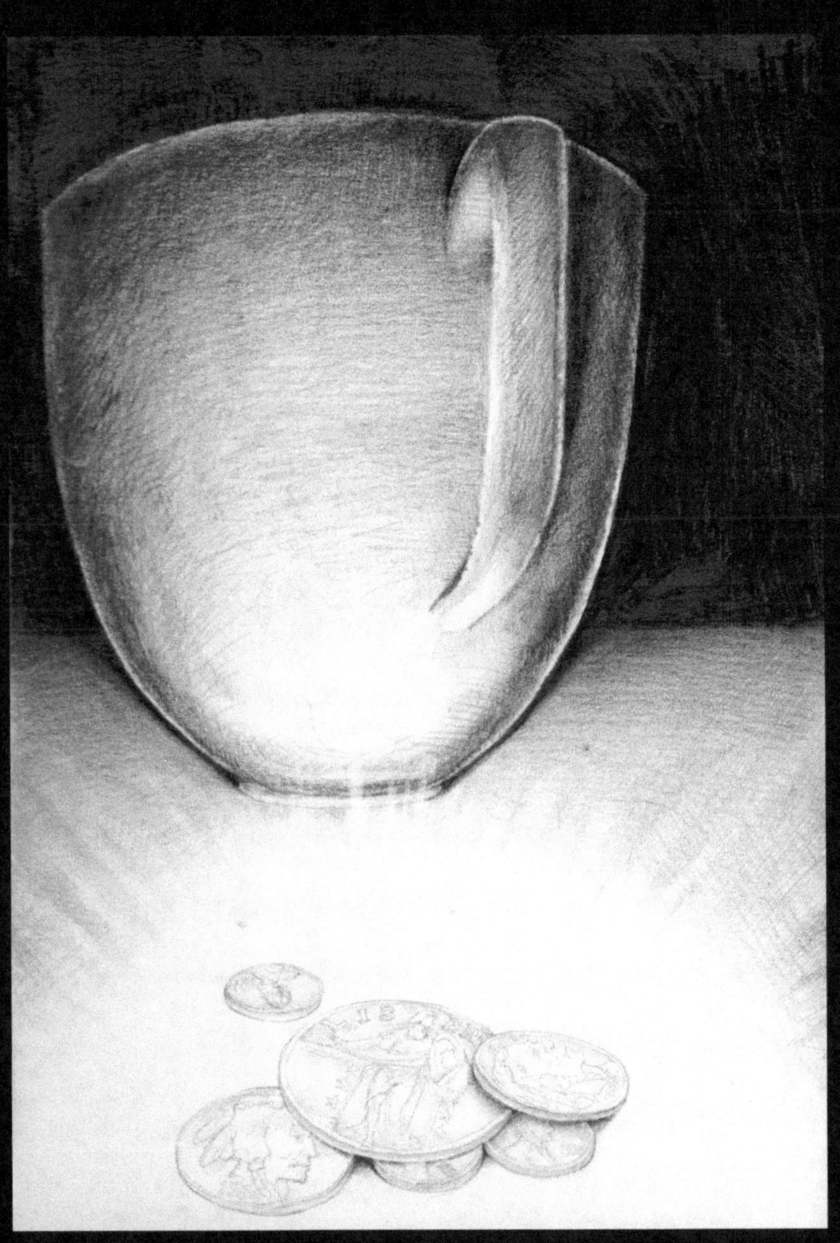

Like the pallor of dead bodies.

# ALLAIGNA'S SONG: ARIA

*JM Landels*

Allaigna's Song: Aria *is the second novel in the Allaigna's Song trilogy by equestrian swordswoman, artist, and editor* **JM Landels**. *Her first book, fantasy bestseller* Allaigna's Song: Overture, *is available from Pulp Literature Press and Amazon. You can follow her adventures with pen and sword at jmlandels. stiffbunnies.com.*

# ᴘREVIOUSLY IN ALLAIGNA'S SONG ...

*Fourteen-year-old Allaigna's ability to sing music into magic has taken a deadly turn when, defending herself from rape, she accidentally kills her betrothed-to-be. With the help of travelling singer and father figure Morran Rhoan, she flees Aerach, still unwilling to return to her family, and still hoping to find her true father. Poor judgement on the road from Werrancross leads the pair into the Sandhorn desert, where they become unwilling guests of the Sidharen people's Sage Clan. Allaigna negotiates their release by taking a blood oath with the Clan leader's daughter, Kîan. Back on the road with Rhoan, Allaigna is no closer to finding her birth father.*

# Verse 23

## Responsibility

**Gleoran, though not as busy as Werrancross,** is a large enough frontier town that Rhoan and I decided it was worth the risk of finding an inn for the night. It no longer felt safe to work as travelling entertainers, so we kept to ourselves. Even though I was of Brandishear blood and had spent a year and a half in its capital, I felt alien in this town. The language was the same, and the customs were the same; under the treaty, Brandishear and Aerach might as well be the same nation. And yet I felt a vast ocean, not a mere sandy desert twenty leagues wide, separated me from my homeland.

As we sat in the low-ceilinged common room of the inn, our heads held low beneath the false ceiling of smoke, I found myself fingering my pendant again, longing to turn it over, gaze into a pool of fresh water, and see if I could hear Angeley's voice calling me.

But I let it drop back inside my shirt, conscious in the dark room of its pearly pink glow and suddenly frightened of drawing attention from the other tenants of the room, or from the Mage Guard. I remembered clearly how much more present those black-robed policemen of all things arcane were here in my grandfather's realm than back home in Aerach. I didn't think so small a magic as this would call their notice, but I couldn't be sure. And the Mage Guard were more active in border towns.

I could feel Rhoan's question before he asked it. I'd been waiting for it for days.

"So where next?"

*Why ask me,* I wanted to say. *You're the adult. I'm just a child.* I so dearly wanted to turn responsibility over to him, or to anyone. But I was barely a child, despite my unfinished form. I was old enough to be betrothed, to have killed a man, to have taken my fate into my own hands. I might as well shoulder the full responsibility. Till now I had been running from the lies my mother had told me, from the life demanded of me, and from the life I'd taken. It was time I started heading *to* somewhere.

Wandering the countryside and hoping to stumble upon my father wasn't working, and I wondered that I'd ever pretended it might. I needed someone who had travelled the borders and knew the Ilvani, and I berated myself for not having thought of her before. I recalled her words to me: "If you ever have need of me, you have but to ask." I had forgotten that promise for years. She could be stationed anywhere, but she was in the Ranger corps and eventually could be found. I looked up into Rhoan's eyes, wondering how he would react, and wondering too why he'd never asked this of me himself.

"We're going to find Rhiadne."

It was not the reaction I'd expected. A smile, some sign of happiness at the prospect of seeing his long-lost love, perhaps. But there was barely a blink. A flicker of something passed behind his eyes, but the rest of his normally expressive face held a mask-like stillness. He took a long drink from his tankard and slowly, fastidiously, wiped the foam from his lips with his travel-stained lace cuff.

"Will she know aught about your father, do you think?"

Taken aback by his cold reaction, I stuttered slightly. "Sh-she's a captain in the Rangers. Who else knows as much about the comings and goings of people in the Ilmar?"

"Indeed. And are not the Rangers the ones we've been avoiding the last few weeks?"

"Yes, but …" I paused, trying to find words to express the muddle in my head. "But Rhiadne would never … I mean, she would understand. She wouldn't turn us over. Not me. Not you?" That at least should have been a certainty, not a question.

"I hope not. At least the girl I knew would not. But I would not ask her not to. Would you ask her to compromise her position by aiding us?"

My heart dropped into my belly. Would I? The old me would have. The child of privilege who felt the world existed to serve her. It rankled that I hadn't recognized the jeopardy I would place her in. That it had taken Rhoan to point it out.

"Of course not." I sank further into my chair, defeated. A lump began to coagulate in my throat as another thought took hold. "I can't—" I paused, swallowing back the lump. "I can't ask you to take any more risk for me either." The smoke had lowered, watering my vision and obscuring his features. I continued. "We should separate. You're not on any handbills of my family's. And we don't even know that anyone is looking for Doniver's … killer."

He said nothing, his face unreadable behind the smoky veil.

I coughed, my throat stinging. "I need air," I mumbled, heading for the inn's rear doors.

The smell of the midden heap at the back of the building was sharp enough to blast the remnants of smoke from my nostrils but did nothing to prevent the continual watering of my eyes. Where to go then, I wondered, if not to Rhiadne? I couldn't conjure up places in this strange country, only names and faces. Garæthiel, Glaignen, Goff. Chal. Even Fîal. It was not my father I wanted, but friends. But what friend could I trust, and what friends would not be in danger from my presence?

I felt small, childish, and alone.

I drew the curved dagger that had once belonged to my father from the top of my boot. The clearmoon was beginning to spill watery light into the stable yard, washing away the dim orange from the inn behind me, replacing it with monochrome hues.

It made the knife look stranger, more alien, and even more deadly. The light was insufficient to see the intricate carvings on the haft, but I could feel them, familiar now to me after sleeping night after night with the knife beneath my pillow. The dagger was more familiar than my sword, or maybe even than my bow. As familiar as the handle of the knife I ate and prepared my food with, as familiar as the reins of Nag's bridle. *Not Nag's anymore,* I corrected myself, fighting with the tightness in my throat once again. And yet, as intimately as I knew the strange weapon, I was no closer to knowing its owner. If there were clues to his identity in this artefact, they were opaque to me, and all my travel and trials had been the aimless wanderings of an errant child.

Aimless, but not harmless. For I'd lamed my horse, killed a man, and caused no end of hardship to Morran Rhoan. I had done some small good too, I appealed to my sterner conscience. I'd shut down the boar-baiting operation, given Raddick his family lands back, and made an alliance of sorts with the people of the Sandhorn. That last, I felt, was rare and new.

So did it matter if I was no closer to finding my father? Could I not walk away from this quest and start my life from here?

I turned the dagger over in my hands. It would feel like giving up. The knife held no visible hints to my father's identity or locale, but it was still my only clue. And it might mean more to others. It had lived hidden in my boot top too long.

I felt a hand on my shoulder and turned to look up into the warm eyes of Rhoan. I knew from my mother's description that my sire was tall and dark-haired like Rhoan. I could only hope he was as kind.

"Will you carry a message for me?" I asked. "To Rhiadne?"

He nodded sadly, hopefully. "Where will you wait for her?" he responded, knowing already what the message would ask.

I hadn't thought that far. The only place in Brandishear I knew was Rheran. It was also the only place large enough to hide me.

I searched my memory for a suitable inn. I had never set foot in one when I was there, so I relied on images of the signs hanging in the street. "At the Red Horse, near Brônagate." I had no idea what the place was like on the inside, but the image of the red horse, my Grandfather's sigil, on a green sign hanging against the blue skies and white stone of Rheran was clear in my head. "Leave word there for … for Deil Taran." It was Ilvani for 'little crow'. "And I will check daily for messages."

Rhoan nodded, neither protesting nor questioning, and it made me suspicious.

"You *will* do this? You aren't planning to merely follow me?"

He was full of wounded innocence. "My word is my troth, Allaigna. If I give it, you may trust it."

I narrowed my eyes. "But you haven't given it yet."

He sighed. "Yes, all right. I was planning to follow you."

I was touched, reassured, and irritated.

"But," he continued, "while you were out here … breathing the night air," he said, wrinkling his nose at the yard's clinging odour, "I made arrangements for you to travel with a caravan to Rheran."

I was furious. How did he know where I'd go before I knew myself? It was almost enough to make me change my plans to spite him. But how could I? It was too convenient, too reassuringly safe, too bloody thoughtful of him.

He smiled. "I know it will cramp your style, sticking to the plodding pace of draught animals, but you'll have food, a place to sleep, and"—the smile grew wider—"the family has pledged to see my daughter safe to her aunt in the city."

"Aunt?" I asked.

"A friend of mine in Rheran. I'll write you a letter of introduction."

I was fuming inside, overcome by irritation that he had arranged all this in so short a time and that it made far too much sense to refuse. And then another of his words struck me.

"Family?" I said. "Is this not a merchant van?"

"Far better." The irritating smile came again as he led me back into the tavern.

"Mistress Dourva," he said as we pulled up three-legged stools beside the table. "This is my daughter, Merri."

I was taken off-guard by her masses of ginger-gold hair, caught back with ribbons, and her eyes. They were green not blue, but nonetheless so like my grandmother's that I had no doubt this woman was Leisanmira.

I took her hand and bowed respectfully, terrified and awkward yet somehow glad to be with my grandmother's people.

# Verse 24

## Blood Ties

**The caravan departed Gleoran** in the orange hours of early morning. Rhoan rode with me to the outskirts of town, where the wagons were rolling into place amid eddies of children, dogs, and goats.

Our shadows stretched towards them, two black spearheads reaching for the colourful melee. I reined in before my shadow horse's ears touched the nearest van. I didn't want to say goodbye with other eyes around.

I didn't want to say goodbye at all, no matter that this parting had been my choice. I had set out looking for a father, and though I hadn't found my own, here was one who had all the qualities I could hope for. But would he even want a daughter, I wondered. Especially one who'd caused him so much trouble? I fought back the water in my eyes, tried to look at him, and failed.

"Allaigna." He so seldom used my name it almost came as a shock. "You don't have to, you know. Go alone."

I shook my head. I would not go through these arguments again, especially when he might win. It was all too tempting to turn away, to go with him in search of Rhiadne or ask him to come to Rheran with me. And I refused to change my mind.

"If you ever change your mind," he echoed my thoughts, "send word. I have no home to offer, but you will always be welcome to travel with me."

I managed to look at him at last, sideways, with the rising sun bouncing circles and shafts of light around his head.

"Thank you," I whispered. It was an inadequate phrase to encompass all I had to thank him for, but it was what I could manage. So I repeated it, reaching out from the saddle to embrace him before our horses shifted away again.

I wiped my eyes on my sleeve, re-ordering my face as I approached the caravans, unsure of where to ride or who to ask. There was no sign of Dourva, but she was probably in one of the wagons. I took a deep breath and approached the nearest outrider. Facing the maddened sow hadn't been as frightening as this.

"Pardon me." I hated how high, thin, and girl-like my voice sounded. "I've arranged with Mistress Dourva. To ride with you—"

The young man turned in his saddle, squinting into the morning sun. I looked down at my saddle bow, nervously adjusting my reins. "I'm—"

"Allaigna?" asked the rider.

I looked up. His face was half-shadowed by the hand he held against the sun's glare, but I recognized the smiling eyes and fox-red hair, three years taller and broader though he was.

"Glaignen?" I stuttered, amazed. Why had it not crossed my mind that he could quite logically be here with a gipsy van?

"But no—not Allaigna. I go by Merri these days."

He wasn't listening. He was off his horse and on one knee beside mine. He placed one hand on my stirrup, the other on his heart.

"My oath, sister, if you'll have it, is too many years coming."

"Get up," I hissed as eyes started to turn towards us.

He stood, so much taller now that his head came to my elbow, but he did not let go of my stirrup.

"I'm happy to see you too," I muttered, confounded by his obeisance. And by his grown-up and admittedly handsome face gazing up at mine. "But I am not travelling under my own name. Please, I beg you, can you keep my secret?"

This seemed to trouble him.

"I owe you my life——"

"You don't," I interrupted, more and more uncomfortable with the attention we were drawing.

"And I have given you my oath. The Leisanmira do not keep secrets amongst themselves. But I will forsake my clan ties if you ask it."

I shook my head, horrified. "No! I don't ask it!" The sudden tumble of words and oaths dizzied me, and I wanted to flee. I turned my horse's head away. "I'll just go." Though with that turning, I was surprised to feel my heart lurch and want to stay.

Glaignen caught my rein.

"Wait, Allaigna ... Merri."

I held, softened by his use of my false name.

"There are no secrets amongst us, but we never let one slip beyond us. Whatever reasons you may have for forsaking your name, you are one of us. By blood, and by my oath. Your secrets are safe with us."

There was a warmth in my chest that threatened to make me cry again. I wanted to relax into the promised safety. I wanted——but was afraid——to release caution.

"Will you at least come and visit my grandmother again? She is old and never leaves her caravan, but it would do her heart good to see you."

I looked with trepidation at the painted wagon I knew to be Nourd's, but I nodded, unable to say no to the welcoming green eyes below me.

As I followed Glaignen to Nourd's wagon, I felt myself shrinking back to the reluctant nine-year-old I was when I first set foot on that step. Even though I no longer needed a hand up, Glaignen was there, as he had been five years ago, with a light and gallant touch on my fingertips, pulling me in behind him.

"Grandmother," he said. "It is Allaigna."

There was no surprise in her reaction. She sat at her table as if she'd been waiting there forever. I shivered. Of course there was no surprise. To Nourd, as to my own grandmother, the future is an open book. She tapped the table with her palm.

"Welcome," came that pebbled voice. "Sit." And then, "Glaignen, you may go."

I turned to look at him, terrified of being left on my own with Nourd. But he smiled, gave a reassuring squeeze of the fingers he still held, and winked before stepping back out into the golden morning sun.

The caravan seemed dark and airless when the door closed, and my heart was hammering as I sat once more at Nourd's table. Her eyes were different, a paler blue clouded with age.

"Come closer," she barked. "Let me see you."

I leaned over the table, nearer the small evenlamp. The flesh-starved fingers of her gnarled hands shot out on either side of my face, pinioning me like a mouse in the claws of a falcon. I didn't dare move or breathe as the bony fingertips walked across my face.

How ironic, I thought, for one with the Sight to lose her vision. As if she could hear my thoughts, she spoke again.

"I see light and dark, but little else with my eyes these days. It has only made the Sight clearer." She dropped her hands. "Why are you here, Allaigna?"

I wanted to shoot back that she should already know that. I shivered again when I realized she already did; my answer was part of a test.

"I'm looking for my father," I replied as evenly as I could, eschewing the padding of courtesy.

"Why?"

I blinked. It was a question I'd never asked myself.

"To … to find out who I am."

"Tt. You already know that. You are Irdaign's granddaughter and Lauresa's daughter. You're a privileged brat of the nobility, but you carry your grandmother's blood."

I bristled. "And what of my father's blood—does that not matter at all?"

"Oh, it matters very much, young Brandis. It matters what you do with it."

I bit back a reply, momentarily confused by her calling me by the name of Brandishear's hero. But of course it was also my grandfather's surname.

She continued. "You don't need to find out who you are. You need to find out who you will be. The bowl." She pointed a bent finger at the brass bowl sitting high on a shelf.

I remembered the bowl. I remembered looking into its water-filled surface as a child and seeing things I neither understood nor wanted to see. I stood reluctantly and retrieved it.

Its sand-scoured surface was thick with dust.

"Wipe it out," she commanded, handing me a faded turquoise scarf, "and fill it." She pointed at the ewer of water on the table.

Reluctant or not, I felt compelled to obey, cleaning off the layers of dust, polishing the dull yellow surface, and at last filling it with rippling clear water.

"I can't use it anymore," she whispered in a hoarse voice that seemed almost sad. "And I don't need to. With the world gone dark for me, I see more than I ever did. But I miss its beauty."

It was beautiful. The scouring pattern created mesmerizing whorls and spirals of gold light that scintillated through the water, even in the dimness of the cabin.

"But," she continued, "I can help you."

My heart was pounding triple-time by now, quailing in unreasoned terror at the thought of looking in those waters once more.

"Come." She put her hands out, palms up on either side of the bowl. "It will show you what you need. Maybe it will even show you your father."

The look on her face was a challenge. Clearly she thought my father would not appear in those waters. That was all the dare I needed.

Straddling the three-legged stool, I put my hands into hers and, like I'd seen Angeley do so many times before, blew into the water.

**When at last I let go,** my limbs were trembling, my body soaked in sweat, and my breath coming in short gasps.

*No,* I thought. *I cannot. I will not.*

Furious, I glared at the old woman. "So—that's it? My future? As if I have no choice?"

"There are always choices." Her voice seemed softer, younger now. "The responsibility, to accept or decline, is always yours.

The future is never fixed until it has happened—and even then is subject to interpretation."

"Why me?" I hissed, the anger still burning hot. And the unspoken resentment: why have you shown this to me? Why have you burdened me with the future, like you and my grandmother have been burdened?

"Why not you? Is there anyone better, more fit? Your brother, perhaps? Goffree? There are many options."

*Not them,* I thought. *Neither is fit.* But I didn't say it aloud. Instead I issued another challenge.

"You said it would show me what I need. I saw nothing to give me direction."

"Nothing?" she asked, her clouded eyes mild.

A memory flicked back, of a man silhouetted against a purple storm-fraught sky. I couldn't see his face. Only the background was visible: the high west tower of the Bastion.

**I paused on the step of Nourd's caravan,** blinking in the harsh morning light that sparkled from the wet brass bowl I held.

It was heavy in my hands, empty of water now but filled with the weight of foreboding. I wanted to let it fall, with all its portents, there on the roadside. Or better, to fling it away. I imagined it sailing through the cloudless sky, flashing in the sun, flinging diamond drops of water in its wake. But I knew I could not. My rebellious heart was still no match for the sense of duty and responsibility trained into me.

I hugged the offending object to my chest, crossing the short-cropped grass almost furtively to where Glaignen stood holding both our horses.

His eyes widened slightly at the sight of the bowl, or perhaps of my glowering face, but he said nothing. I opened my saddlebag to find room for the bowl and then paused, turning it over in my hands.

"This should be yours," I said thoughtfully, congratulating myself already on handing off the unwanted gift. "I don't have the Sight. I can't use it, but you —"

He held up both hands in refusal.

"Nor do I."

I shook my head, puzzled. "But you do. I remember …"

"No longer," he smiled, no trace of regret in his eyes. "It's rare in boys to begin with. And unlike womenfolk who grow into it, it fades in us when we grow up."

"I'm sorry —"

"Don't be. It's a gift, and useful one at that. But it's also —"

"A burden," I finished for him.

"Aye." He put his hands around the bowl, not taking it from me but rather holding it in my hands. "One I'd take back if I could. But its time with me is over."

"I don't want it," I whispered, not sure if I meant the bowl, the Sight, or the destiny I'd seen.

"You will cope," he replied, gently pushing the vessel back against my chest.

I nodded dumbly, feeling dread seep into me as if from the scoured brass.

"We'd best mount up," he said. "The vans are moving."

Indeed, the colourful wagons had started their creaky roll forward, shifting into line on the road. Our horses swung their hindquarters nervously, anxious not to be left behind. I put the bowl in my saddlebag and mounted as my pretty Sandbred mare danced beneath me.

# VERSE 25

## BROKEN TIES

**Glaignen kept me amiable company** as my horse pranced and fretted behind the slow wagons. I wanted to relax and enjoy the ride on this beautiful late spring morning, a fine horse beneath me and a handsome young man beside me. But I felt chains around my heart, anchored with the weights that rode in Nourd's caravan ahead of us. The light was too bright, the mare's pace too jiggly, and I felt my head start to pound with every stride.

I answered Glaignen's pleasant attempts at conversation with the briefest of replies, eyes cast down at my horse's neck, the tension running through my back and hands making her all the more choppy and difficult.

Waves of nausea began sloshing in my stomach, and when the caravan stopped at noon to let the horses rest, I retreated beyond the roadside and threw up my breakfast into the bushes. I stayed there, resting my head on my knees even while the van started to move again.

Glaignen, of course, came to find me.

"Go on ahead," I told him. "I'll catch up."

"What do you take me for, that I'd leave a maid in distress by the roadside?" His words were light-hearted, but I could hear concern beneath them, which only annoyed me.

"Please. Just go." I didn't want to throw up again in front of him.

Instead he swung down from his horse and sat beside me.

"Two can catch up as easily as one. I'll wait for you to be feeling better."

If my head hadn't hurt so much, I would have yelled. Instead I gritted my teeth, kept my voice low.

"Thank you. But I don't want company."

The hand he placed on my back made my soft shirt feel like a horsehair blanket on my oversensitive skin. I shrugged it off, trying not to vomit again or to cry with the throbbing pain in my head. I reached into my shirt, pulled out the eversweet posy I kept with my pendant, but even that sharp clean smell would not clear my head.

I heard his breath, felt it like a hot desert wind.

"You still wear it."

He meant the pendant. The one he'd given me five years before at the Autumn Fair, when we'd first met. That was the first time I'd had a headache like this one, and sudden suspicion filled my head. I tore it off my neck, its absence feeling cold and naked on my skin.

I wanted none of it: no gipsy magic that chained me to prophecy and made my head ache.

I scrambled onto my horse's back, reached into the saddle bag, and pulled out the bowl. My throat was too full of tears to speak, to explain, to apologize, or even to breathe.

I spurred my horse, and as she filled the air with dust, I threw the bowl to him. It looked just as I had imagined, spinning and flashing in the sun as I galloped away south.

**He followed me for some time,** I think, but my desert mare was faster and could run longer than his draft cross. As I fled from friends, obligations, and responsibilities, the Valnirata Greatwood edged my vision to the left: a deep green ribbon both mysterious and frightening, which called to me like the Eastern Forest had at home.

But to the right, the rich fertile fields of Brandishear opened, welcoming and warm, also my home by birthright. Through the gilded haze of nostalgia, the two years I'd lived there seemed the best of my life.

The two landscapes pulled on me equally, leaving me no place to go but straight ahead. I'd never travelled in Brandishear and knew only Rheran and its environs. But Rhiadne was stationed on the south-eastern border. And Morran Rhoan was heading there to find her. The thought of them both made my heart beat a little slower, my stomach unclenching.

And then I stopped, jerking my mare to a rude halt from her ground-covering trot. *No.* I didn't need another family. I already had one father too many, and if I couldn't find my real one, I wanted no other. As for the rest of them — well, I'd had enough of the tangled weave of love and lies.

My head was pounding worse than ever now, and I had no desire to be sick again. I slid out of the saddle and leaned against the trunk of an aged oak, welcoming the shade. A small sheep enclosure bordered the track, though no farms were nearby.

Barely able to stand, I untacked my mare and let her into the field to graze, while I sank down beneath the hedgerow and closed my eyes to the world.

# Verse 26

## Token

**A summer rain was falling** as I walked up Rheran's high street.
Not cold, but damp and dispiriting nonetheless. I had stabled
my horse at the Red Horse Inn, where I'd agreed to meet Rhoan,
but had left no message nor taken a room. I was filled with an
uneasy restlessness, light and directionless. I found myself at
one point in front of Goff's grandmother's house and wondered
if I should inquire within. But we'd not parted as friends two
years ago, and regrets over my recent encounter with Glaignen
clouded my thoughts.

And then there was Fraell Edris. I could take my dagger to
her—see if she, with all her sword lore and contacts, could
trace its descent. Or Garæthiel. I could send a message to the
Bastion to see if she or Fîal would care to meet me. But the
Bastion seemed most frightful of all, its grey stone base rising
wet and grim from the crown of Rheran Hill.

I turned back down Clealla Way, away from the high street,
and found the Greenling Hostel. It was an overflow barracks
used when Brandishear's troops were called in and could not
all be housed in the Bastion. Between times, many rangers and
troops on leave preferred it to quartering in the castle anyway. It
was closer to the nightlife of the city and less scrutinized than
the entries into the well-guarded Prince's seat.

For some reason it appealed to me as well, better than the well-appointed inn frequented by visitors to the city. I left my mare at the Red Horse, though. Her presence there would tell Rhoan or Glaignen I'd arrived safely. But I paid in advance and left no other address. When I decided to meet either of them again, it would be on my terms.

My money was running low, so I agreed to sing in the evenings at the Greenling to pay for my bed, leaving my weapons with the hosteller for security.

I had been there four or five nights, singing in the evenings and reacquainting myself with the roads and alleys of Rheran by day, with no sign of either Glaignen or Rhoan. I don't know if I was disappointed or relieved to delay all contact with people I knew, but I checked back on my horse daily, just long enough to groom her and give her carrot ends from the Greenling's kitchen or a last-season's apple.

I left the hostel that morning, carrot tops in hand, after retrieving my father's dagger from the innkeep. I didn't wear my sword but decided, after an encounter with drunken youths the day before, that a small show of arms was prudent.

With the dagger thrust prominently through my belt, I stepped into the already hot morning only to be jerked roughly back into the dark of the hostel by an arm through mine.

I yelped in surprise before a hand was clamped over my mouth. I reached for the dagger, but it was across my body, and my other arm was twisted upward so painfully I had no choice but to follow.

"Sh," said a voice in my ear. "Apologies, but you shouldn't go outside with that."

I looked up and over my shoulder, eyes readjusting to the dim light once more. I recognized the man. He'd been in the hostel a few nights already while I'd performed, chatting with friends, carousing with a chestnut-haired woman who was obviously more than a friend. I could see the emblem on his cloak — a Brandishear Ranger — and began to squirm.

"Hst! I won't hurt you, girl! Stop fighting me and sit down."

He pushed me, not so gently, into a chair and sat down beside me, boxing me in a corner between a table, a wall, and him. My dagger, I noticed, was in his hands. I opened my mouth to protest and he shushed me again.

"Where did you get this?" he asked.

There was such urgency, such menace in his question I didn't dare dissemble.

"It … it was my mother's."

"Was?" His fingers spasmed on the handle of the knife, clenching it with whitened knuckles so the tip curved toward me.

I flinched backward, pressing into the corner.

"Is?" I amended.

"And your mother is of what House?"

I swallowed, unable to comprehend the question at first. Like an idiot I finally stuttered out, "She's not. Not Ilvani."

"You do know it's death for an Ilmari to carry a blade such as this?"

I stayed silent, staring into his cold-eyed glare like a rodent facing a hawk.

"If you believe that sort of thing," he added, releasing the dagger so it spun on the table, settling with its handle pointed towards me. "I do know any self-respecting *dreimar* would kill you just for touching it."

A small flame of defiance rose up in me.

"Not that it's any of your business, but my father gave it to her."

"And where did he get it?"

"I don't know. I'd like to find him and ask." I looked up into the chilly eyes, not daring to question or hope that this man, the first to know something about the weapon, might know something of my father as well.

He shook his head slowly. "Best not, child. Do you know what this is?" He didn't wait for an answer. "An Ilvani blood blade. No two are alike." He traced the intricate carvings with a long finger. "Each one is forged for a particular vengeance. This one has already been used."

I shivered. "How do you know?"

He ignored the question. "If this was your father's, then he stole it. Take it back if you would, but if I were you, I'd keep it hidden. Even here in Rheran's walls there are those that would kill you just for looking at it."

My hand hovered over it as if the grip would brand me if I laid hold of it again. I breathed, let my fingers settle on it. It didn't burn at all but felt cool and familiar in my hand.

"Stolen or not, it's all I have of him," I said.

"Oh, I doubt that," he said, smiling. It was no more than an upward twitch of the corner of his rod-straight mouth, but it softened his face, made it almost handsome in a thin and weathered way. "I'm sure you have something of him. His eyes, perhaps. His chin? His hair?"

I wanted to know more—to find out what this stranger knew of the knife, but I couldn't find a way to ask.

"Did you assault me just to issue this warning, sir?" I asked instead as I tucked the knife back into its old, hidden spot beneath my tunic.

Another twitch of a smile. "No one makes a career singing in barracks on purpose. You seem to lack direction."

He pushed away from the table, stood. "In two day's time there will be what we nicely call a recruitment drive. Most of the idle youth of the city will find opportunities to serve their prince. I'd suggest you leave by then if you don't wish to be press-ganged into the infantry."

I thought at first he mistook me for a boy, then remembered again we were in Brandishear, where women also could be pressed into military service.

"Or," he continued, leaning down to place a round wooden token on the table, "show them my chit and you'll be posted to the Sixth Rangers. It's not an easy life, but it's better than that of a foot soldier. Or a beggar."

I sat, turning the token over in my fingers after he left. It was stamped with BRVI on one side and the mark of a raven's head—the emblem of the Sixth Rangers, I guessed—on the other. I thought of my pendant—the one I'd worn so long and ripped from my neck a mere two weeks before—with its red foal and black crow. I'd lost my horse, my posy, my pendant. All I had left were my weapons: sword, bow, and dagger. I had forsaken magic and the bends and twists of prophecy. Why not turn to the simple life of a ranger? Spend time in the forests and wilds that had called to me all my life? I'd be alone for the most part, but when in company, I'd be with others like Rhiadne, my most admired mentor. And then there was the stranger who had more, perhaps, to teach me of the knife I carried.

Or I could wait for Glaignen or Rhoan. Either of whom would take me back like family. Or take me back to my family, if I asked.

**I knelt,** one of at least two hundred new recruits, in the courtyard of the Bastion and made my oath, once more, to my grandfather. I kept my head down, not wanting to meet his eyes in case he recognized me, then rose and made my way through the throng to join my captain.

§

*This brings us to the end of the final instalment of* Allaigna's Song: Aria. *Look for the release of the complete novel, including one-third previously unpublished material, in September 2019 from Pulp Literature Press.*

*You can't escape magic when it's in your blood ...*

When Allaigna was seven she almost sang her baby brother to sleep — forever. She may not be heir to her mother's titles and secrets, but she has inherited her grandmother's dangerous talent for singing music into magic.

*Allaigna's Song: Overture* is a love story, a family saga, and a coming-of-age novel that braids together the stories of daughter, mother, and grandmother.

*ISBN: 978-0-9949565-9-0 (print)*
*ISBN: 978-1-98886500-3 (eBook)*

**Epic fantasy bestseller on amazon.ca**
**Pulp Literature Press**

# THE ARTISTS

### AKEM
*Cover artist*, Greetings

Akem forgot she was an illustrator and writer for a few years and is making up for lost time. Her first picture book, a myth about before we were born, is in progress. Her painting *Seabus* was the cover for *Pulp Literature* Issue 16, Autumn 2017, and *Windseeker* graced the cover of Issue 18, Spring 2018. You can find more of her fantasy illustrations at akemiart.ca.

### CHAILLE STOVALL
*Illustrator*, 'Wall Street at Night'

Chaille Stovall is an award-winning American director and illustrator whose passion for creative problem solving and artistic career began at the tender age of nine years old. Chaille is a conceptual thinker and director known for his diligence in preserving literature and the human experience through the media of visual and performing arts. His films, *Boyz in Tights*, *Party Animals*, and *Little Monk* received numerous awards and international recognition and feature figures such as the Dalai Lama, Jimmy Carter, George W Bush, Philip Seymour Hoffman, and Al Gore. He was also a guest speaker at the 2002 TED conference with speakers Yo-Yo Ma, Richard Dawkins, and Frank Gehry. By the age of fifteen, *People* Magazine named him one of '20 Teens Who Will Change the World'.

In 2016, he began attendance at Sequential Artist's Workshop's one-year program, where he gained mentorship from comic book masters Tom Hart and Justine Anderson, and he is currently developing new work to expand into visual translations. Stovall currently resides in Gainesville, Florida, and creates content for his company, Multiverse Productions with his partner.

## Mel Anastasiou

*In-house illustrator*

Mel Anastasiou loves drawing for *Pulp Literature* because she loves the stories she illustrates. She draws in black and white, working from imagination and inspired by details from Renaissance compositions. You can find more illustrations, as well as writing tips and news about her books and novellas, at melanastasiou.wordpress.com, and see her artwork on Facebook at Bird and Branch Artwork.

# HALL OF FAME

# MARKETPLACE

## Books

**Advent** *by Michael Kamakana* • We thought we knew what the aliens wanted. Think again. • pulpliterature.com/advent

**Allaigna's Song: Overture** *by JM Landels* • Music, magic, and the shaping of a hero. • pulpliterature.com/allaignas-song-overture

**The Labours of Mrs Stella Ryman: Further Fairmount Mysteries** *by Mel Anastasiou* • Trapped in a down-at-the-heels care home. You'd be cranky too. • pulpliterature.com/stella-ryman-and-the-fairmount-manor-mysteries

**Paperboy: A Dysfunctional Novel** *by Bob Thurber* • Photography by Vincent Louis Carrella • shantiarts.co/uploads/files/thurber_paperboy.html

**What the Wind Brings** *by Matthew Hughes* • Epic slipstream historical fiction • pulpliterature.com/product-category/novels/matthew-hughes

**The Writer's Boon Companion** *by Mel Anastasiou* • Thirty Days Towards an Extraordinary Volume • pulpliterature.com/subscribe/the-bookstore

## Bookstores

**Book Warehouse** • 632 Broadway W, Vancouver, BC V5Z 1G1 • 604-872-5711 bookwarehouse.ca

**Myth Hawker Travelling Bookstore** • Canadian authors • Canadian content • small and independent press • mythhawker.ca

**Phoenix On Bowen** • 992 Dorman Rd, Bowen Island, BC V0N 1G0 • 604-947-2793

**Village Books & Coffee House** • 130-12031 First Ave, Richmond, BC V7E 3M1 • 604-272-6601 • villagebooks@shaw.ca

**White Dwarf / Dead Write Books** • 3715 10th Ave W, Vancouver, BC V6R 2G5 • 604-228-8223 • whitedwarf@deadwrite.com

"*Myth Hawker has a crush on the underdog: the small press, the overlooked author, the independent bookstore, and the vast, undiscovered treasures of small-scale publishing.*"

**Myth Hawker travels the length & breadth of Canada, popping up at conventions & festivals in every province, showcasing the work of small press & independent Canadian authors. Follow them online to see where they're popping up next!**

**www.mythhawker.com     @Mythhawker**

# Because every issue is an EVENT.

# Read. Subscribe. Submit.

- 2018 Journey Prize Long-list
- 2017 Canadian Magazine Awards Winner, Best Literature and Art Story, including Poetry
- 2016 National Magazine Awards Finalist, Fiction and Personal Journalism
- 2015 National Magazine Awards Finalist, Poetry

# eventmagazine.ca

# Do you have a **story to tell?**
# We can help!

Dreamers is dedicated to heartfelt writing. Visit our site for:

- Therapeutic Writing
- Poems & Stories
- Content Marketing
- Creative Nonfiction
- Writing Workshops
- Contests & Anthologies
- Residencies & Retreats
- ...and so much more!

**www.DreamersWriting.com**

The Digest Enthusiast
Book
June
Tom Brinkmann
Steve Carper
Peter Enfantino
Vince Nowell, Sr.
James Reasoner
Robert Snashall
Joe Wehrle, Jr.

MARCH 2019
MYSTERY WEEKLY
Magazine
FICTION BY
C. L. Cobb
Martin Zeigler
Gregory L. Norris
Gina Burgess
Stan Dryer
BV Lawson
K O'Connor
by Mike McHone

MORE THAN A MAGAZINE - WE'RE ALSO A LOT OF MERCHANDISE!
(BUT WE'RE ALSO A GREAT MAGAZINE!)

GO TO STORE.AMAZINGSTORIES.COM

AMAZING STORIES

AMAZING STORIES

AMAZING STORIES

ALLEN STEELE'S CAPTAIN FUTURE IN LOVE
AMAZING STORIES

POLICE PUBLIC BOX

AMAZING

AMAZING STORIES

# Dear Geist...

I have been writing and rewriting a creative non-fiction story for about a year. How do I know when the story is ready to send out?

—*Teetering, Gimli MB*

Which is correct, 4:00, four o'clock or 1600 h?
—Floria, Windsor ON

Dear Geist,
In my fiction writing workshop, one person said I should write a lot more about the dad character. Another person said that the dad character is superfluous and I should delete him. Both of these writers are very astute. Help!

—Dave, Red Deer AB

# Advice for the Lit-Lorn

Are you a writer?
Do you have a writing question, conundrum, dispute, dilemma, quandary or pickle?

*Geist* offers free professional advice to writers of fiction, non-fiction and everything in between, straight from Mary Schendlinger (Senior Editor of *Geist* for 25 years) and *Geist* editorial staff.

# Send your question to advice@geist.com.

We will reply to all answerable questions, whether or not we post them.

geist.com/lit-lorn

GEIST

FACT · FICTION · NORTH of AMERICA

# MICHAEL KAMAKANA

# ADVENT

WE THOUGHT WE KNEW WHAT THEY WANTED
WE WERE WRONG

# CONTESTS

*Pulp Literature* runs four annual contests for poetry, flash fiction, and short stories. For contest guidelines, prizes, and entry fees, see pulpliterature.com/contests.

The Raven Short Story Contest
**Contest opens:** 1 September 2019
**Deadline:** 15 October 2019
**Winner notified:** 15 November 2019
**Winner published:** Issue 26, Spring 2020
**Prize:** $300

The Bumblebee Flash Fiction Contest
**Contest opens:** 1 January 2020
**Deadline:** 15 February 2020
**Winner notified:** 15 March 2020
**Winner published:** Issue 27, Summer 2020
**Prize:** $300

The Magpie Award for Poetry
**Contest opens:** 1 March 2020
**Deadline:** 15 April 2020
**Winner notified:** 15 May 2020
**Winner published:** Issue 28, Autumn 2020
**Prize:** $500

PULP
Literature
Become a member!
Join the Pulp Literati today
pulpliterature.com/join-pulp-literati

# $\mathscr{B}$ecome a Patron of Pulp Literature

By supporting *Pulp Literature* on Patreon with \$2 or more per month, you will be laying the foundation for a secure future for the magazine, as well as ensuring that you never miss an issue! Your subscription includes four big issues of short stories, novellas, poetry, comics, and novel excerpts, delivered to your door or electronic mailbox each year. **Find us at patreon.com/pulplit**

If you prefer to subscribe through our website, go to pulpliterature. com/subscribe.

Or you can send a cheque with the form below to
*Subscriptions, Pulp Literature Press, 21955 16 Ave, Langley BC, V2Z 1K5, Canada*

---

*Don't miss an issue!*

❑  **Send me 2 years (8 issues) at the special rate of \$90** (save \$30)*
❑  **Send me 1 year (4 issues) for \$50** (save \$10)*
❑  **Send me 2 years of digital issues for \$30** (save \$9.92 )
❑  **Send me 1 year of digital issues for \$17.50** (save \$2.47)

Name: _______________________________________________

Address: _____________________________________________

City: _______________________________ Prov. / State: _________

Postal code: ______________ Country:______________________

Email: _______________________________________________

❑  **Payment enclosed**
❑  **Bill me**
❑  **New**
❑  **Renewal**

Make cheques payable in Canadian funds to J. Landels. Include email address for digital editions and Paypal billing, or subscribe at www.pulpliterature.com.

*for postage outside Canada add \$20 per year in North America or \$36 per year overseas.